# After the scrum.

## DAHLIA DONOVAN

*After the Scrum* © 2016 by Dahlia Donovan

*After the Scrum* is a work of fiction. All names, characters, events and places found therein are either from the author's imagination or used fictitiously. Any similarity to persons alive or dead, actual events, locations, or organizations is entirely coincidental and not intended by the author.

For information, contact the publisher, Hot Tree Publishing.

www.hottreepublishing.com

Editing: Hot Tree Editing

Formatting: RMGraphX

Cover Designer: Claire Smith

ISBN: 978-1-925448-09-2


10 9 8 7 6 5 4 3 2 1

# Dedication

*For all those struggling to be who they are*
*in a world that isn't often kind.*

# Glossary

*After the Scrum* is written in British English and has a colourful collection of colloquialisms and slang. Enjoy discovering some new and wonderful terms.

Bobbies: Police officers

Frotting: Unexpected rubbing of your crotch against someone.

Mo: Slang for moment

Morn: Shortened version of morning.

Narky: To get irritated.

Nutter: A crazy person

Poncey: Someone who is pretentious or affected.

Prat: An idiot, but a less offensive term.

Scoffing: To eat very quickly

Scrum: A rugby term. An ordered formation of players used to restart play, in which the forwards of a team huddle together to gain possession of the ball.

Telly: Television

Tosser: Slang. A person who masturbates. Used as an insult.

# Chapter One

*I'm retired. I am retired. I've retired. I'm a former rugby player. And I'm bloody talking to myself like a bloody moron. This is not a good sign.*

Stretching his six-foot-one, bulky body, Caddock Stanford unfolded himself from his favourite leather recliner. He could no longer afford to pretend his career hadn't come to a painful end. The English national rugby union team no longer looked to the Brute for direction on the pitch.

For almost eight years, Caddock had been the star on the front line of the scrum. He'd been playing since he was a lad, since his hands were first big enough to hold a ball. Nicknamed "the Brute" for his total lack of fear and his raw power when ploughing through the other side, he'd led his lads to victory an impressive number of times on the national team.

Only a few days before his fortieth birthday, Caddock had suffered one tragic loss after another. It started with news of his younger brother, Hadrian, dying in a tragic accident while scuba diving. Haddy had been a marine biologist—and a father of one bright four-year-old boy.

So many lives changed in one instant. Caddock had experience as a *brilliant* uncle who spoiled little Devlin Stanford rotten. He'd never been a father, had no desire to be one. Yet now his nephew had become his sole responsibility.

As if his life hadn't been flipped on end enough, it had taken one hit to his knee in training before a World Cup game to bring his stellar career to an abrupt halt. The doctors believed the Brute would never enter a scrum again. They'd advised against him even attempting it.

The worst part of it all—his knee was fine. It didn't bother him at all 90 percent of the time. But the doctors feared another hit could render him crippled for life. His manager hadn't been prepared to take the risk.

Shouldn't it have been his decision? Caddock had argued pointlessly with anyone who would listen. He'd still found himself kicked out on his arse. Legends apparently had an expiration date, and his had come due.

The world moved on without him. No one had time for a former champion, no matter the number of titles behind his name. The Brute would be a faded legend mentioned in anecdotes by pundits, but nothing more. No amount of raging at the wind would change any of it.

Forty. Retired. And a father. Now what? The infernal question rolled around in his mind and kept him up late at night. Devlin deserved the best care one could provide. A moping mountain wouldn't do the lad a damn bit of good. He needed a restart—a scrum—to deal with life after rugby.

Starting towards the kitchen to make a coffee, Caddock sighed when a familiar voice called out, "Uncle Boo!" Since Devlin started to speak, he'd tried to teach the lad to call him Uncle Brute. It backfired spectacularly when he became a bastardized version of his own nickname.

*Uncle Boo.*

*Bloody Boo.*

"Uncle Boo. *Uncle Boo*. Uncle Boo." Devlin bounced into the kitchen clutching his favourite blue teddy to his chest. He'd clung to it as the last toy his father had given to him before his trip to the Great Barrier Reef. He waved the bear wildly, almost knocking himself over with his enthusiasm. "Blue wants bickies."

"Does he now?" Caddock crouched down to contemplate the bear seriously. "Custard or chocolate biscuits?"

"Choccy." His little nephew grabbed his hand to tug pointlessly at him, trying to drag him towards the cabinet where his favourite biscuits were hidden on a top shelf. They'd been moved up there when he discovered the little devil could climb just about anything. "Pwease?"

"Oh no, not the magic word." He lifted the boy up to sit on the counter. "Just one now. We're having tea and sandwiches in a mo."

"Thwee."

"One."

"Two."

"One." Caddock had learned to be firm when sad blue eyes peered up at him. Devlin could melt a bloody iceberg with his pout. "And a half."

Devlin gave him a wide toothy grin, though he was currently missing two of those teeth. He immediately shoved the entire half into his mouth. "Thank you!"

While his nephew munched on the promised biscuit, Caddock glanced around his cramped flat with a sigh. He'd been happy in his home as a single bachelor. It simply didn't work as well with a troublesome lad who seemed to come with three times the mess.

Never mind the rubbish schools in the area, his nosy neighbours, and the occasional visit from bored journalists on slow news days. They needed a change. A new start for both of them would be just the thing.

His dad wanted them to move closer to home in Sheffield. *Not a chance in hell.* He loved his parents dearly, but they seemed to think him incapable of tying his own shoes. They also differed greatly on the best way to raise a child.

They argued fiercely about Caddock's lifestyle choices.

Or at least, something his father believed to be a choice. They'd agreed to disagree, mostly to avoid upsetting his mother. She was the one little Devlin had inherited his sad eyes from.

Caddock had been at his wits end for weeks. He had so many things to consider. He'd finally decided to fulfil one of his lifelong dreams—owning his own pub. The dream of just about every retired rugby player he knew.

A former teammate ran a real estate agency in Cornwall. Caddock had called in a favour with him. After a month of searching, they'd found a quaint seaside village that fit the bill perfectly.

*Louie?*

*Lou?*

*No, Looe, that's it.*

His mate had made it sound perfect for his purposes. It was on the small side with a relaxed, open community, with good schools and a pub available for purchase. He'd offered to purchase it and a nearby cottage instantly.

Caddock had never been one for waiting around to make a decision. A tug on his sleeve had him glancing down to find bright blue eyes peering up at him over the furry head of a teddy. His eyes narrowed on the innocent smile.

"Blue wants a stowy." Devlin held up the bear as if to prove his case.

Caddock gave a mournful glance towards the telly; his team were playing their rivals in a derby. *Damn it.* He tried briefly to reason with his nephew. "Are you *certain* he wants a story right now?"

"Pwease?"

"Go pick a book then."

*And the sad eyes win again.*

The things one did for one's nephew. The weekends were usually spent with the two together, joined at the hip. It was another reason to consider life in a small village. His nephew could flourish there without the expectations of others, including his grandparents.

While reading about Peter Rabbit for the thousandth time, Caddock went through his internal task list. Moving with a four-year-old would be tricky, especially one whose life had been thrown into chaos by the loss of his parent not so long ago. He'd have to be sensitive.

*I can do sensitive.*

*Right?*

Devlin had lost his mother very early in life. She'd suffered heart failure, owing to a defect that had remained undetected. The young lad was as resilient as all children tended to be. He deserved happier things... happier memories.

When Haddy had named him godfather to his son, it had been a bit of a shock. Caddock, at the time, was more known for drunken nights, broken hearts, and the occasional broken nose. Why would anyone voluntarily choose to trust him with a child?

Yet his godson seemed to give him a reason to change. Those clear blue eyes had stolen his heart. It had caused him to make a complete overhaul of his life—less drinking for one thing.

His brother had been his son's hero. Devlin had idolised his father in the way little boys usually do. Caddock had rather large shoes to fill, and he wanted nothing more than to prove himself worthy.

"Devil?" Caddock closed the book and set it to one side. Time to have a chat. He turned his nephew around in his lap so they were facing each other. "Remember when I talked about us maybe moving to a bigger house? Would you like to live by the sea in a cottage?"

"The sea?" Devlin's eyes went wide. "Like Toad and Mole?"

Caddock gave a deep chuckle before nodding. "Well, more sea than river, but yes, just like Toad. Might be a nice change for us."

"And sandcastles." Devlin bounced excitedly while rambling off a list of things one could do by the sea. He finally slowed down, tiring with a wide yawn. "Wanna go to the sea, Uncle Boo."

"Right, then. The sea it is." He ruffled the boy's dark brown hair, something all the Stanford males had inherited. His unfortunately had turned grey earlier than anticipated. His brother had often teased him about dyeing it. "Maybe after a nap."

"No nap." Devlin yawned for a second time. He was already half-asleep by the time Caddock tucked him into his bed.

*Right, no nap.*

After settling the boy down for his nap, Caddock fired off a note to his realtor—Rupert Hodson. They were supposed to be signing papers in the next few days. The pictures of the pub and cottage made it seem like perfection.

He could do this. Be a father. Run a bar. He could be something other than a bruiser on a rugby team and a drunken fool.

He could.

The first step would be to stop talking to himself like a

fool. It was a sign of sanity to question one's sanity, right? And it was *definitely* time to take a nap of his own, if only to silence his own mind.

# Chapter Two

FRANCIS

"No, Sherlock, stop it. You uncivilized mongrel!" Francis Keen, interior decorator extraordinaire, tripped over his own feet and his dog's leash. He landed in a heap on the walk outside his home. "Damnation, you obstinate creature, heel. Do you even know what the word means?"

"Having trouble, love?"

"No, Gran." Francis straightened himself up, running his fingers through his now thoroughly mussed-up mass of light brown hair. He ignored his beloved grandmother's tittering giggles while attempting to glare balefully at his Shetland sheepdog, Sherlock, his beloved and the bane of his existence.

"Have a good day, Gran."

"Try to stay on your feet, love." She waved at him with another laugh then headed up the walk to their shared home.

*Oh, the humiliation.*

He'd gotten a smaller dog to go with his own more slender frame. He didn't fancy being dragged off by a monster of a mutt. Sherlock didn't appear to understand his purpose in life. Even for a smaller dog, he managed to yank his owner off his feet quite frequently.

The sheltie served other purposes, besides companion and best friend. Francis simply didn't advertise what Sherlock's training actually entailed. He didn't want the sympathetic stares.

"One morning, Sherlock, just one would be nice. I'd give you the largest beef bone in the world if you could allow me to preserve my dignity once." Francis fumbled with the keys to his only prized possession—a turquoise Fiat 500 from the seventies that had been painstakingly and lovingly refurbished. He patted the dashboard reverently once he'd situated himself and his insane canine. "Well, Watson, time to take the world by storm. Are you ready?"

Francis had grown up in Truro. His parents died in a car crash not long after his seventh birthday and he'd been with his grandparents in Looe ever since. At twenty-five, he still lived with his gran.

She'd tried to toss him out on his ear, but Francis feared leaving her by herself. His granddad had died after a fall in the cottage—alone. He didn't want gran to suffer the same fate.

Staying with her was comfortable and familiar. Gran didn't

badger him to *man up* like so many of his teachers had done over the years. His eccentricities were simply what made her grandson who he was—or so she told him.

Life in Looe might not have the excitement of London, but the village had mostly embraced Francis. He decorated many of the local businesses during the various holidays. He also threw on the occasional new coat of paint here or there.

"No chasing after Mrs Tinkles." Francis warned Sherlock when he started to bark at his nemesis. "We promised to behave. Remember? The butcher might chop you up for stew if you go after his wife's cat again."

At eighteen with a scholarship in hand, Francis had left the village to prove himself. He'd graduated with a degree in interior design from Regent's University in London. It had been a start, but he'd never truly found the big city a fit for him.

The only thing London had given him—aside from a degree—was a broken heart. A boy his age named Trevor had stomped all over his fragile feelings. It had sent Francis running back to Cornwall, tucking his metaphorical tail between his legs.

Trevor had been his first love. It had felt as if the world were coming to an end at the time. He still cringed whenever he thought about the man.

After sobbing into his gran's cream tea and scones for a month, Francis had followed her advice to start his own design firm. In just a year, he'd built a decent business, and since kept all of his energies focused on work.

Love.

Well, love hadn't shown back up in his life. Gran kept telling him to "go out, love, go snog some bloke." He usually nodded in agreement then ignored her advice completely.

Francis figured Sherlock and Watson were companion enough for him. Did it matter that one was a dog and the other a car? He ignored the rhetorical question and pulled up outside of his tiny office space, cramped between a tea shop and a bookstore.

"Mornin'."

Francis waved to Ruth who owned the tea shop and bakery. He graciously accepted her bribe of fresh-baked custard tart. He gave her a knowing look; she usually gave him the broken ones for free, not the best ones. "What happened now?"

"My Stevie put his elbow into the willow platter." She glared over her shoulder to her gentle giant of a husband, who stood sheepishly in the shop doorway. He shrugged at the both of them. "He does mean well. Do you think you could you find another one?"

"I'm going on another antique hunt this week. I'll keep an eye out," Francis promised. He shook his head when Ruth slipped a peanut butter biscuit to Sherlock who sat obediently in front of her. "I'll bring it by when I find one."

Working in a little village, Francis found himself more often than not playing antique hunter or painter rather than actual designer or decorator. His work would never grace the covers of design magazines, but it had a unique joy all its own.

Carefully balancing his leather bag, the custard tart, and the leash, Francis made his way up the narrow stairs to the cramped space he called an office. He tossed his bag to the side, released Sherlock from his leash, and started up his computer. Dragging the curtains open to let in light, he prepared himself for another day in Looe.

*Boring, but safe.*

He kicked his shoes off and sat cross-legged in his office chair, coffee mug balanced on one knee with the custard tart on the other. He batted away Sherlock's curious nose as he tried to sniff out the pastry. "My treat. You had three peanut butter biscuits, you don't need my tart."

Sherlock sniffed at him before retreating to the massive pillow on the floor nearby. He curled up on it and plopped his head down on his paws. Francis chose to ignore the mournful gaze being sent his way. He was made of sterner stuff.

*Maybe a biscuit wouldn't hurt?*

Francis tossed one to the incorrigible creature then started to munch on his custard tart while perusing the multiple emails in his inbox. He deleted the messages offering to increase the size of his gentleman's bits. Did people even believe those things? The ones about Xanax and a prince in some country who needed a loan followed shortly after.

It was always disappointing to start out with fifteen new messages, yet end up with only four that required a response. And worse, only one actually appeared to be about a new client. It seemed the old pub by the butcher had finally been purchased. The new owner needed someone to help with the décor of it, along with a cottage down by the sea.

Interesting.

The rumour mill had yet to pick up on this. Francis would finally have something to share with his Gran over tea in the afternoon. She always loved to gossip with him about everything she'd learned in her visits to her friends around the village.

Firing off a quick response to the realtor, Francis started pulling together a few ideas for the pub. He'd visited it a few times before the previous owner died at the ripe old age of ninety-one. It *definitely* needed to be brought into modern times. The seats were practically falling apart, never mind the peeling paint and cracks in the ceiling.

A village like Looe could attract crowds during the holidays, but aside from those times, it was a quiet place with mostly locals and others from nearby who'd frequent a pub. The villagers wouldn't want to visit a pretentious modern pub.

He tossed aside some of the samples and moved on to a more traditional vibe. He held up a swatch of fabric to his snoozing sheltie. "What do you think, Sherlock?"

*Yawn.*

"Not a fan then? Me either." Francis moved on to the next one. "How do you think he'll feel about tartan? Yes, I agree, he'll hate it."

Yet another day spent talking to his dog.

*I am going to die alone—surrounded by antiques and a dog.*

# Chapter Three

CADDOCK

A knee to the stomach and an excited "Uncle Boo!" had *not* done anything to improve Caddock's mood when he awoke early Monday morning. He gently plucked a bouncing Devlin from his chest and set him on the bed. A quick peek at the alarm clock informed him that he had at least two more hours to sleep.

"Go make breakfast." He grunted sleepily to a giggling Devlin. "I want a full English."

"Uncle Boo." Devlin leapt up onto his chest again. "Want awfuls."

"I'm confident you mean waffles." Caddock caught the small, pointy knee before it could connect with his stomach again. "Listen, Devil, how about you go put on something other than Iron Man pyjamas? Hmm?"

"'Kay." Devlin hopped on his uncle one last time before dashing out of the room.

"Caddock 'the Brute' Stanford taken down by a four-year-old's pointy limbs." He groaned, sitting up while rubbing his chest gingerly. He'd taken to sleeping in a T-shirt and shorts since Devlin took a fiendish joy in dive-bombing his uncle by way of an alarm. "I'm too bloody old for this shit."

"Naughty word, naughty word." Devlin's giggling voice drifted down the hall with the light patter of running bare feet.

Naughty words meant whipped cream and berries with his "awfuls." Caddock rolled out of bed and shook his head with a groan. He scrubbed his fingers over his greying dark brown hair, cut short enough he didn't have to worry about it getting mussed up, even at night.

Stumbling into his bathroom, Caddock glared at his reflection in the mirror while leaning tiredly against the sink. He looked haggard and aged. The move would hopefully allow him a chance to truly relax.

A little village like Looe might be a bit of a risk. Would they be able to blend into a much smaller population? Did it matter that sports pundits still nattered on about him on occasion? *God, I hope not.*

"AWFULS!"

"It's waffles, you deranged child." Caddock dragged a clean shirt over his head, shifting it to fit over his muscled chest. He made his way quickly towards the kitchen to prevent a four-year-old's meltdown over breakfast. "Strawberries?"

# After the Scrum

"Yeah." Devlin nodded so vigorously he tipped forward on the stool that he'd climbed up on. He giggled when his uncle caught him. "Thank you."

Pouring him a glass of juice to stay him over, Caddock began the process of making waffles for breakfast. Taking on his nephew had forced him to take a crash course in cooking. Before now, the best he could manage would be toast with eggs that slightly resembled scrambled.

The girl at the bookshop thought him mad when the six-foot plus rugby star had purchased fifteen cookbooks. He'd never had to cook for the lad before, but kids couldn't eat takeout all the time. His mother had offered to come stay with them for a bit.

It was a generous offer, a kind one even, but not a chance in hell would he agree to it. His mother meant well. She truly did. Her help generally involved making him feel like a ten-year-old again with a skinned knee and mud on his nose.

So after many, many long nights of reading cookbooks and burning his way through a few pots and pans, Caddock could manage most of the basic recipes. He'd never be a brilliant chef. Devlin didn't need him to be a gourmet. Avoiding poisoning the both of them would be sufficient.

"Can we go to the sea now?" Devlin asked around a mouthful of waffle, cream covering his chin and part of his cheek. "Pwease?"

"Already?"

Making up his own plate, minus the cream and berries, Caddock dropped down in a chair beside his nephew. They ate in relative silence for a few minutes before Devlin couldn't resist asking about the sea again. Four-year-olds weren't generally known for patience.

Rugby brutes weren't generally known for patience either. They'd blame it on the patriarch of the Stanford family. He blamed his dad for a ton of other things, why not impatience?

While Devlin raced off to clean his hands and face, Caddock turned his attention to the message from his realtor. It seemed a local designer, Francis, would be taking on redoing the slightly dilapidated pub and nearby cottage. She'd already sent over samples for his approval.

Bird had good taste. The paint, fabric, and antique ideas in the photos from the email fit perfectly with his concept for the pub. It wasn't too modern, but didn't appear like something from some bizarre period film either.

Better to not tell his parents about the bird though. They'd start trying to set him up with her. He wanted a decorator, not to be shoved into a relationship with someone from the wrong gender.

Sighing into his coffee, Caddock decided to leave *that* line of thought for another day. His father seemed to particularly enjoy arguing rather loudly with him about it. It was yet another reason to move further away from them.

His parents meant well, but tended to have rather strict ideas about raising children. They'd been tough on him and Hadrian. Devlin was a good boy who only needed a bit of freedom combined with guidance.

"Uncle Boo?"

He barked out a laugh when Devlin appeared by the corner of his desk in swim trunks, holding his little sandcastle bucket.

"Where you going with those, then?"

"The sea." His nephew hopped up and down, swinging the little orange pail around in his hand. "You pwomised."

"Did I?"

Devlin nodded fiercely. "After awfuls."

"*Waffles.*"

"'S what I said." He blinked up at his uncle in confusion.

Caddock covered his face with his hand, torn between laughter and a groan. He hadn't planned to travel to Cornwall so soon. "How about next Saturday?"

"No."

The sounds of his favourite cartoon on the telly provided a suitable distraction for the little Devil. The idiot box gave a brief respite from the numerous questions that plagued the parents of all four-year-olds. It gave him time to text with Rupert to settle the details more concretely.

If they were heading that direction, it might be wise to see if they could also visit the pub and cottage. Devlin had a week off from school, after all. He deserved a break. The salty sea air would do wonders for the both of them.

Rupert promised to have not only the deeds ready, but the decorator at the pub for a meeting. If they drove down today or tomorrow, the two could scope out the new village and the beach. His nephew would be over the moon at finally being able to build his sandcastles.

A moment later, his thoughts were interrupted by a little devil clambering into his lap. His nephew's blue eyes filled with tears as he admitted to missing his dad. Caddock wrapped his arms around the distraught child. No words could heal his loss. They'd have to continue to weather the occasional emotional storms together as best they could.

"I miss him too." Caddock rested a gentle hand on the boy's tousled hair. He rocked back and forth until the lad's breathing evened out. "I'd bring him back if I could."

"Is he in 'eaven with Mum and angels?" Devlin turned serious, watery blue eyes up at him. "Stevie says only the bestest people go there."

"Well, your dad was the best man I ever knew. Better even than me." He ruffled the chaotic brown curls while his nephew giggled. "Tell you what, how about we drive down to Cornwall today?"

"The sea!"

*And thank God for resilient children who are easily distracted.*

# Chapter Four

FRANCIS

*"Sherlock!"*

The muffled shout didn't accomplish anything while Francis struggled to kick Watson's rear door shut. His arms filled with all manner of supplies, others clamped between his teeth, while he stumbled up the path to the pub door. His irrepressible pup darted helpfully around him, making it impossible for him to navigate over the threshold without banging into several chairs and careening to the floor with a loud clatter.

"Thanks, Sherlock." Francis flopped over on his back to stare up at the ceiling. His head rested on a stack of fabrics. He intended to pick out one set for curtains and another for upholstery on the new chairs. "Why'd you have to be allergic to sheep? Why couldn't you be allergic to being a nuisance?"

"How do you know he's allergic to sheep?" A deep, almost raspy voice queried from further back in the bar.

It might possibly be the most orgasm-inducing voice

Francis had ever heard. A deep, gravelly timbre with only the barest hint of an accent. He'd wager the man attached to it would be large—hopefully in all the best ways.

"So?" How'd you know he's allergic?" Mr Orgasmic Voice prompted impatiently, disrupting Francis's wild fantasies.

"I asked him."

"You asked him? Are you mad?" His footsteps moved closer.

"Only on Sundays." Francis sat up and slowly inspected the stranger from the tips of his dark blue trainers up his large, denim-covered thighs, across his broad chest and muscled arms, to finally rest on the handsome face attached to the impressive body. A rather familiar face at that. He'd know those clear blue eyes, slightly bent nose, and short greying hair anywhere. "You're the Brute."

"*You* watch rugby?"

"Sweaty and muddy men in tight shirts and shorts grappling with each other?" Francis batted away Sherlock's attempts to lick his face. "Who wouldn't watch it?"

A long silence followed that was only broken by the sound of Sherlock's nails on the scuffed wooden floor. Francis wondered if perhaps he'd embarrassed the large man. Some people seemed to find his *openness* offensive—poncey pricks.

"Not to be rude, but what're you doing in my pub?" The Brute, or Caddock Stanford, glared fiercely at him.

"Francis Keen." He held out his hand, amused by the difference between the rugby player's massive grip and his own slender one. "I'm your interior decorator."

"But…" The man looked at him, utterly bewildered, still

holding on to his hand. His hold tightened ever so slightly before letting go. "You're a bloke."

Francis glanced down at himself in mock horror, even lifting out his cardigan to glance at his well-defined but slight upper body. "Am I? This explains so much. No wonder the women screamed when I went into the wrong loo the other day. Well spotted, you man detector, you."

Caddock's brow furrowed deeply before he burst into deep, raucous laughter that was as sensual as his speech had been. His oversized mitt of a hand squeezed Francis's shoulder once. They didn't get a chance to speak further as Sherlock herded a small child out from behind an overturned table.

He blinked in surprise between the boy and the Brute. "He didn't come with the pub."

It earned him another glorious laugh and an introduction to young Devlin—nephew and godson apparently. Francis sensed a less-than-happy story, so made a quick gesture to Sherlock who pranced around immediately. It worked to lighten the mood. Caddock sent him a grateful smile over the oblivious head of his giggling four-year-old.

"Rupert gave me a spare key to start working." Francis gestured towards the menagerie of items still scattered across the dusty floor. "You approved of my vision for the space?"

An abrupt nod was the only response. Maybe the Brute was the strong silent type? Francis found his mind drifting to all the ways to elicit sounds from the stoic man who'd clearly suffered several losses outside of just his career recently.

Wouldn't it be lovely to lick a path down his thick neck? *Oh, yes, please.*

*Think non-sexual thoughts,* Francis urged himself while his body responded to the sudden visuals in his mind. *Think about Gran in the shower. Oh, bugger me silly. I'm traumatized for life. Bleach my brain.* He shook his head then smiled sheepishly at the man who watched him worriedly while waving a hand in front of his face.

"Sorry, sorry," Francis stammered apologetically. He twisted around to face anywhere but in the direction of the man who had way too much of an impact on his composure—and libido. Rupert had been right—he really needed to break his streak of bad dates. It had clearly been too long since his last romp in the sheets. Lusting after a straight, unavailable man wouldn't do anything for his battered heart. "I—"

"Uncle Boo. *Uncle Boo.*" Devlin bounded over with Sherlock happily circling around him. "Can I has a puppy too?"

*Uncle Boo?* Francis mouthed the words, watching the two in the reflection of the dirty bar windows. His heart melted at their interaction. For all his aggressiveness on the rugby pitch, Caddock seemed more gentle giant than anything else with his nephew.

"Maybe Mr Francis will let you play with Sherlock every once in a while when we've moved to Looe? I bet he would if you asked nicely." Caddock managed to redirect his nephew with what appeared to be practiced ease.

"Can I? Can I? Pwease?" Devlin turned powerfully pleading eyes in his direction. "I can take him for walkies. I'll be good. I pwomise."

Francis glanced with a sense of inevitability between the

child and his own manipulative dog who had sad brown eyes of his own. "Of course you can. Sherlock would love to have your company."

With a cheerful shout, Devlin danced away with the traitorous sheltie beside him. The pair played tug-of-war with a fabric sample. Laughter and happy barks filled the pub and put smiles on the faces of the men watching their antics.

"Those blue eyes are dangerous. He'll be a heartbreaker when he's older." Francis started to gather up everything from the floor. He mentally added cleaning to the top of his to-do list, freezing in place when Caddock knelt to help him. *Act calm, Keen, act calm.* The Brute's eyes were just as dangerous as the little lad's. Time to distract himself. "Were there any changes to the design plans you wanted? Have you decided on a name? There's a great place that makes those old-fashioned wooden signs if you have."

"Haddy's."

"Haddy's?"

"For my brother, the Devil's father." Caddock's eyes dimmed with hurt and the faintest shimmer of tears, which disappeared after a few quick blinks. "This is a new start for us."

Francis felt suddenly emotional for this strong man life had clearly battered around a fair bit of late. He rested his hand on Caddock's forearm briefly. "Looe's a brilliant place for starting fresh. Oh, and Ruth makes the best custard tarts. Don't eat them on Fridays."

"Why?"

"Her husband, Stevie, makes them and he's rubbish at it."

He gave a wry smile. "The village is a fantastic place to raise a young lad."

Caddock cleared his throat with a harsh cough, turning his attention to Sherlock. "Does your dog herd anything if he's allergic to sheep?"

"People."

"People?"

"Yes, people." Francis nodded to where Sherlock was clearly guiding Devlin's path. "He's rather devious about it as well."

# Chapter Five

Margaret Keen was a wise old woman and Francis had learned at a young age never to underestimate his gran. She had a *keen* sense of when something had happened to her beloved grandson. It was something he generally tried and failed to avoid.

He'd never managed to sneak something under her nose without being caught. It had been a source of frustration for him, and amusement for his granddad. The two often commiserated on her almost magical abilities to ferret out secrets.

"You've met someone."

Francis studiously ignored his gran's knowing looks. She'd been teasing him for days, as he'd drifted around in a mildly befuddled stupor after meeting his new client. He'd avoided telling her *why* he'd been so glossy-eyed. "No, I haven't."

Her eyes narrowed on him while Francis made a show of adding a thin layer of marmalade to his toast. They were noshing at the tiny table in the kitchen. It was the warmest room in the house in the mornings when the bitingly cold breeze drifted off the sea.

It had been a tradition with his grandparents, as long as Francis could remember. Breakfast before school at the table, he'd treasured the time with them. He could admit to himself he now clung to his gran—afraid to lose the last of his family.

"You've *met* someone." She tapped her spoon against his plate to get his attention. "You get all wide-eyed and put too much sugar in your tea when you start fancying someone new."

"*Gran.*" He briefly reconsidered all his earlier mushy thoughts about her. "Must you torment me before I finish my tea and toast?"

"You've finished your tea, now stop avoiding my question." She leaned across the table to stare pointedly at his mostly empty cup.

"Must run. Don't want to be late for a new client." Francis crammed his toast into his mouth and dashed out of the room. "Later, Gran."

Her laughter followed him through the house while he snatched up his leather bag and snapped his fingers for Sherlock to follow. His trusty Fiat sat outside, waiting for them both. Mornings like this were the only time regrets about not living on his own taunted him.

Most of his friends had places of their own, far away from their families. Or at least, they weren't in the same block, let alone the same house. But it didn't feel right to leave Gran on her own.

"Well, Sherlock?" Francis opened the door for the sheltie to hop into Watson. "Think we can manage to avoid utter humiliation today?"

Sherlock barked then twisted around to lie down in the passenger seat with his head resting so he could look out the window.

"Not sure if that was a yes or a no." Francis tossed his bag in the back and slid into the driver's seat. "Maybe the Brute will have left already?"

Another bark.

"Thanks for the support." He scratched Sherlock behind the ear. "Maybe Ruth will have biscuits."

Ruth *did* have peanut butter biscuits—and a slightly squished pain au chocolat. It seemed Stevie had managed to get his elbow into a couple of pastries while they were proofing. She'd saved them for Francis.

Life in Looe would always be slightly left of centre. Francis tended to be slightly off-kilter much of the time as well, so who was he to complain? He chuckled to himself while heading up to his office to check messages before heading to Haddy's Pub to really start fixing it up.

"My desk is *not* a chew toy." Francis frowned at Sherlock when he gnawed briefly on one of the antique legs. "No, stop it, blasted mongrel. I paid five thousand quid for this thing."

Sherlock tilted his head and barked. *Useless creature.* Deciding not to risk any more of his furniture, Francis grabbed the printouts of his plans for the pub and headed out the door. He could walk down the few blocks to the bar, giving his overly enthusiastic sheltie a chance to run himself at least a bit ragged.

He rarely bothered with a leash. Sherlock had become something of a fixture in the village. He regularly visited most of the shops, begging for treats and attention.

"Be needin' any help with the pub?"

Francis found one of the *less* friendly villagers blocking his path. "No, but thank you."

"You sure?" Patrick "Patty the Drunk" Edwards leaned in closer, giving him a full view of rotted teeth and breath to match. "Could use a few quid to tide me over."

"Quite confident." Francis attempted to edge around the man with Sherlock pressed firmly against his leg. The dog always stayed close to him when his anxiety started to rise. "Have a good morning."

Holding his breath, Francis quickly strode down the pavement and up into the pub. He slammed the door. Once inside, he slid to the floor with his back against the closed entrance. Sherlock clambered up into his lap, resting his head on his owner's shoulder.

The panic attacks had started when Francis lived in London. He'd been young and idiotically believed himself invincible. A few drunks outside of a gay club in Vauxhall had taught him a rather bitter lesson about the dangers of alcohol and being out of the closet. They'd cornered him in an alley and beaten him rather badly.

He'd avoided clubs and alcohol ever since.

"How humiliating." Francis groaned with his face pressed against Sherlock's fur. His therapist had suggested a dog to help with the panic attacks. The sheltie had been specifically trained to recognize the signs. "Thanks, little love."

For all his often manic energy, Sherlock had taken to his training well. He knew precisely how to soothe away Francis's anxiety. Once the initial panic faded, the sheltie would lick Francis's face and dance around like a clown until he laughed at least once.

Francis's smile turned into a grimace when he noticed the muck covering his jeans from the uncleaned floor. "Well, Sherlock, pub won't clean itself. Can I use you as a dust mop?"

Sherlock barked twice and scampered away from him.

"I'll take that as a no." He chuckled at the dog's antics then got to work. "Floors first, yeah?"

# Chapter Six

Every. Single. Night.

Every. *Single*. Blasted. *Night*.

The same dreams had woken him in a sticky mess for the past week since the visit to Looe. It was all a bloody pain in the arse. Never mind him being too damn old for dealing with things he hadn't dealt with since his teen years.

Caddock had things to do. Lots of them. Moving his and Devlin's lives to a little village required a fair amount of work. He did *not* need distractions. Nor did Caddock have time to deal with sleepless nights caused by increasingly lurid fantasies about his interior designer.

# After the Scrum

*Why now?*

After years of mostly not dating, his life had seemed to reach a comfortable state of loneliness. With a high-profile career, it had been impossible to settle down for anything outside of a few nights here and there. And now? Who wanted a washed-up rugby player with a kid in tow?

The impending move to Looe had his entire routine scrambled. And early morning wet dream wake-ups were less than ideal. All the extra wash was a pain, for one thing. For another, he didn't stand a chance with Francis.

Younger men didn't often go for greyed men like him, unless they had particular needs. Caddock had no interest in playing a role for anyone. It would be best to put the dreams and the man out of his mind—though far easier said than done.

In a short period of time, the movers had managed to help him pack up the furniture and almost everything else being taken down to Looe. The only items left in his now barren flat were clothes and more personal things, which he preferred to take himself. They would easily fit into his Range Rover.

After taking stock of his bedroom, Caddock decided to check on his nephew. It was getting late in the day. He chuckled when he spotted the lad napping on a stack of folded clothes near an open suitcase.

Lifting the snuffling little boy into his arms, Caddock carried him into his own room. They would be sleeping on mattresses for the night. *Indoor camping.* They'd set out for Looe in the morning, following the last of the boxes going with the movers.

His parents had initially wanted to be there to help pack

and then drive to Looe with them to help unpack. It had taken an hour to convince them to stay at home. The last thing Caddock wanted was his lovingly overbearing mother and his perfectionist father hovering over him. Better to have them visit once everything was situated.

Three hours later, with the clock moving ever closer to two in the morning, Caddock finally finished up. He stretched out cautiously on the airbed, hoping it wouldn't pop from the weight of his bulky muscles. He breathed a tentative sigh of relief when it held.

Then the dreaded sound of hissing air echoed in the room. *Sodding piece of shite.* The mattress slowly squashed underneath him until it was completely flat. Caddock lay on the floor and gave an aggrieved sigh.

*Why me?*

He regretted having all the furniture moved first. Sleeping on the floor wasn't ideal for him. What felt like ten minutes later, a small body catapulted onto his chest. Bare feet dug into his abdomen while small hands patted his face repeatedly, all accompanied by periodic giggles.

"Wakey, wakey, eggs and bakey." Devlin sang the rhyme his father had always sung to him. "Up, Uncle Boo, time to get up."

"I'm feeding you to the Loch Ness monster the first chance I get." Caddock grunted when Devlin accidentally kneed him in the stomach. "In tiny pieces."

After a rushed breakfast and a long drive, the two found themselves standing in the midst of a mess of cardboard boxes and furniture. The four-bedroom cottage had more room than his flat, but at that moment, it seemed chaotic and cramped. Maybe they should've asked for help after all.

Once Devlin's room had been straightened out, Caddock left him to play. It took him close to five hours to gain some semblance of organization to the jumble of belongings. He'd emptied a fair few boxes and gotten the kitchen set up by the time his little Devil demanded, "Cheese sammiches and bickies."

Devlin sat on a chair with a sandwich in one hand and a biscuit in the other. He swung his legs, rambling about all the things he would do after lunch. "Gonna see Lock and the sea and Fwannie, and make sandcastles."

"Frannie?" Caddock had no idea how the interior decorator would react to being gifted a moniker by his nephew. "Francis, I believe was his name."

"Fwannie."

"Stubborn as a mule, just like your father." Caddock gave a bittersweet laugh at the pouting child. "Go on then, wash your face and we'll tackle some more boxes."

"Uncle Boo!"

Narrowed eyes had a laughing Devlin dashing off to clean up. *I still got it.* Caddock shook his head at himself. He dumped the dishes in the sink then turned to look at the rest of the, as yet, unopened boxes.

Maybe a break was in order.

He collected Devlin, who whooped for joy, and the two went for a walk in their new village. The cottage was a short distance from the pub and most of the other establishments in the main part of Looe. His nephew seemed particularly excited about the bakery and a nearby bookstore.

"Lock, Lock." Devlin raced forward before Caddock could stop him. He had to jog after the lad, who scampered down the pavement to where Sherlock sat outside the lone coffee shop in town—clearly waiting for his owner. The little boy dropped down beside the dog. "Lo, Lock."

Caddock couldn't bring himself to reprimand Devlin for running off without him. The boy sat, playing happily with the exuberant sheltie. The two had clearly decided they were fast friends.

Francis stepped out of the shop with a cup of coffee and a paper bag in his hands. He blinked in surprise. "Well, hello there."

"Fwannie." Devlin waved enthusiastically at the stunned man who kept mouthing "Fwannie?" repeatedly. "Can I walk Lock?"

With a nod and a wink once Caddock had agreed, Francis fell into step with him, letting the dog and his boy skip ahead in front of them. Caddock watched Francis out of the corner of his eye. He seemed... tired—more than he'd been the last time they'd seen each other.

"Have you...?"

"The pub..."

They started to speak at the same time then stopped with wry chuckles. Caddock motioned for Francis to continue. The younger guy filled him in on the progress in the pub— refinished floors, fresh paint, a thorough cleaning and a new sign to be delivered at the start of next week. It was impressive how much he'd accomplished within just a few short days.

Francis explained that the hardest part, the actual design of the place, would take a bit longer. He seemed to be a perfectionist when it came to his work, not satisfied until the pub fit the vision he'd had for it.

Stopping at an enclosed park, they watched Devlin chase Sherlock around in companionable silence. Caddock enjoyed spending time with someone over the age of four. He'd let himself be too caged up since his forced retirement. Maybe Looe would be more than simply a change of environment for him.

"Rupert mentioned you went to university with his brother." Caddock felt Francis beside him tense up. His old rugby mate hadn't mentioned any uncomfortable history between them. In fact, the realtor had sounded incredibly fond and protective of Francis. "You met in London?"

"I knew them before, but yes, essentially,"—Francis's hands clenched around the bag he held—"Graham, Rupert's brother, roomed with me for two years at university. He's a good friend; both of them are really, though I see Rupert and his wife, Joanne, more frequently."

Caddock sensed the tension that continued to grow and was surprised when Sherlock suddenly abandoned play to come sit at Francis's feet. "You all right?"

"Fine." Francis's fingers drifted into Sherlock's fur, absentmindedly petting him. "I should get back to work."

With a wave to Devlin, Francis wandered off before Caddock could say anything other than goodbye. He took his nephew by the hand to lead him home to their cottage. The mystery of Francis could wait for another day.

"Why's Fwannie sad?" Devlin tugged on his sleeve until Caddock lifted him up into his arms. The lad dropped his head tiredly onto his uncle's shoulder. "We could get choccy bickies for him. I like Fwannie."

In Devlin speak, that meant he liked Francis's dog. Caddock let him ramble about 'bickies' while he thought over the afternoon. He'd give Rupert a call later to pry for information.

"Bickies make me happy." Devlin broke into his thoughts. "Can I have one?"

"Just one?" He gave a low laugh at the quick nod he received. "When was the last time you had only *one*? Is it possible for you to have only a single yummy chocolate biscuit?"

Devlin held up two fingers. "Can I have two?"

Caddock threw his head back and laughed at the little man, who glared at him. "Yes, little Devil, I think you can have two with your tea. How about we pick some fresh ones up at the bakery?"

The exuberant "Yes!" deafened Caddock in one ear. It was still ringing slightly when they stepped in to meet Ruth, the bakery owner. She immediately plucked Devlin from his arms and began showing him all the best bits of the day's baking. All his attempts to pay for the treats were waved off by the woman.

"Welcome to the village, love." Ruth handed him a small basket and ushered the two of them out the door before he could attempt to pay once again. "You keep the little one wrapped up. It'll be chilly by morn."

## After the Scrum

They were definitely *not* in London anymore. Caddock found he didn't miss the overly polite stiltedness of his former neighbours. Looe had a friendly charm to it.

Welcome home, indeed.

# Chapter Seven

FRANCIS

Rupert and Graham Hodson were fraternal twin brothers who had grown up a village over from Looe. Francis had known them by name through his granddad, who was best mates with their granddad. He'd become friends with both while in college. They'd been the ones to pick him up and dust him off after the incident at the club.

His friendship with Graham had been strained by his relationship with Trevor. The two had hated each other almost from the moment they were introduced, and Francis had felt caught between his lover and his best friend. He'd foolishly believed taking his boyfriend's side to be the best decision, though mostly, he'd tried to stay out of it.

The strain hadn't stopped Graham from coming to his rescue. When Francis had been attacked outside of the club, Rupert and his brother had pulled him away from the rampaging drunks. He tried not to think about what might've happened if they hadn't been there.

The two had tended to his wounds, both physical and emotional. Both brothers spent hours with him, ensuring Francis didn't sink into a dangerous depression. Rupert had been the one to suggest the therapist once his panic attacks surfaced.

Time might've passed, but their friendship remained strong. Graham travelled frequently for his consultancy work. It had left Francis in the background, so to speak, though he never begrudged his friend's success.

Every so often, Francis missed the closeness of living with a best mate. They'd roomed together until after university. It certainly involved less nagging, for one thing. His gran might be brilliant—and bossy—but she also had a tendency to want to arrange her beloved grandson's life to fit her idea of perfection.

He shook his head, drawn back to what had started him down memory lane—the panic attacks. Francis found his entire life dramatically affected by them at times. Sherlock made them barely manageable.

"Francis, love?" His gran knocked on the passenger window of his Fiat, causing him to start in surprise. "You coming inside? Or will Watson be your inn for the night?"

"Funny, Gran, simply hilarious," he grumped half-heartedly, realizing he'd been sitting in the parked car for nigh on an hour. She'd never let him live this down, not a chance of it. "I might've gotten a tad distracted."

"Distracted? About what or whom? Want to tell me about him?" She gave him an incorrigible grin that reminded him rather painfully of pictures of his dad. The two shared the same mischievous smile. "Francis?"

"It's been a long day, Gran. How about I make tea and beans on toast?" Francis headed off her enquiry. He wanted space to think without being confronted about anything that might remind him of the unattainable Caddock. "And no, Gran, I haven't met anyone."

Instead of their nightly ritual of tea, scones with blackberry jam and whatever happened to be on the telly, Francis claimed a headache and slunk off to bed. Sherlock curled up at his feet while he stretched out on top of his quilt. He stared up at the ceiling, trying to tune out the sounds in the hallway.

Gran did *mean* well. She truly did, but her hints tended to be about as subtle as a ref's whistle in the ear. Or a whiff of the strongest cheese imaginable.

Everyone in their small community meant well. They always tried to set Francis up on blind dates, fobbing him off on their cousins, friends, even a perfect stranger once. He'd been ushered in front of every available man within a twenty-minute drive. They'd even tried to set him up on a blind date with a woman once.

What was Francis supposed to do with a woman? They had weird jiggly bits. It was all rather terrifying.

"What am I going to do, Sherlock?" Francis kept his voice low.

He often talked to his sheltie, who never offered unwanted advice, making him the perfect listener. "Caddock... he's perfection. How am I going to see him in the village and not melt into a puddle of aroused goo?"

Sherlock shuffled up the bed until he could rest his head on the pillow. Francis laughed at his spoilt-rotten furry friend. He listened to the rhythm of his breathing as Sherlock drifted off to sleep. It lulled him into a light doze while he set thoughts of Caddock aside for the moment.

Maybe it wouldn't be as bad as he feared after all?

Sleep, unfortunately, refused to play nicely. His dreams kept drifting into the steamy sort. Nothing but naked, firm flesh taunted his attempts at a restful night.

Rolling out of bed, careful not to dislodge his deeply sleeping dog, Francis made his way quietly through the dark house. He tiptoed into the kitchen to make a pot of tea, munching on a leftover scone while the kettle heated up. Tea might not solve *everything*, but it couldn't hurt.

Cup in hand, Francis made his way into what had once been his granddad's office. He eased into the familiar, ancient leather chair to soak up the smell of worn leather and old books. It always made him feel safe.

The images from his dream still hadn't quite faded. They'd be featuring heavily the next time he got around to pleasuring himself. Caddock *would* play an unfortunately prominent role that would make it impossible to forget about him.

Several sips of tea helped calm his mind, heart, and arousal down. This whole thing presented him with a rather sticky problem, and not the one in his pants, either. As a professional, it wouldn't do for him to be getting hard in front of his client every time they were in the same room.

*And how humiliating would that be anyway?*

Francis could just imagine the conversation now. "Pardon me while I adjust myself in my trousers." Caddock would likely be unimpressed and definitely not amused. It certainly wouldn't encourage him to give a good reference for future business.

At worst, Francis might end up with a fist to the jaw for his troubles. He'd seen straight men do worse things when they felt their manhood threatened. But Caddock didn't necessarily seem the sort to resort to violence, no matter his reputation on the rugby pitch.

The real question to answer was could he manage to act *normal* around the man? Would his attraction be too much of an issue? It wasn't like he was a complete slave to his desires.

Francis decided his granddad had been right, late-night tea should be spiked heavily with alcohol. He simply couldn't bring himself to drink any of it. The memories liquor triggered were unpleasant at best.

He sank down into the leather chair with a sigh. Being alone wasn't all that bad. He had his gran.

*I have my gran?*

*Oh, saints preserve me.*

It was definitely time to go out on a date. If his subconscious had started to consider his current life as fine, Francis was in more dire straits than he'd initially believed. Maybe another blind date? What could it hurt?

His mind immediately went to the *last* date that had ended

spectacularly dreadfully. Francis might hover on the border of effeminate, but it didn't make him weak. The man he'd been set up with seemed set on treating him like a delicate princess.

It had ended with Francis dumping an entire bowl of mushy peas over the idiot's head. A serious chat had followed with all the well-meaning matchmakers. They'd promised to leave him be—for now.

He could be happy with just Sherlock, and many nights spent watching rugby. Right?

# Chapter Eight

Devlin's introduction to his new school had gone brilliantly—
in the lad's eyes. Caddock hadn't quite enjoyed it nearly as
much. All the little boys in particular had clambered for
his attention, looking with a bit of jealousy at the Brute's
nephew. With luck, it wouldn't lead to any issues between the
classmates.

Leaving the teacher to her work, Caddock headed home to
continue the process of unpacking, slogging through box after
box of useless items he'd collected over the years to finish up
with his office, the only room left. He decided to take a much-
needed break. It wouldn't do to lose all his energy.

# After the Scrum

Tea, fresh air, and perhaps a pastry called his name. It had only taken him a week to get everything in the house situated, outside of his office. They'd settled into village life rather easily, though with Devlin in school, it would be the true first test for both uncle and nephew.

The short walk to Ruth's bakery cleared his head, despite the gloomy, drizzly rain. The cheeky baker slipped him several peanut butter biscuits and custard tarts. It seemed Francis had missed his mid-morning tea break.

*"How tragic. Could you be a dear and take this to Francis? He's so slender, the wind might blow him away this winter. Be a good lad. He's only down the street at your pub. Works so hard that one."*

Caddock found himself bustled out the door and on the way to the pub before realizing he'd paid for *two* cups of coffee, not one. *Pushy, interfering bint.* He'd been avoiding Francis. It hadn't helped with the dreams.

What could one visit hurt?

To his surprise, the pub was empty. The turquoise Fiat sat parked outside, but Francis and his ever-present shadow Sherlock were nowhere to be found. It worried him slightly.

Where were they?

A quick glance around the room showed the continued progress in the refurbishment project. The pub had gone from dusty and dilapidated to pristine in a scant few weeks. It looked like the perfect sort of seaside place that gruff fishermen might've once frequented.

The wooden floors had been painstakingly restored before being stained and then aged to a rich mahogany that matched the bar itself. The walls had been painted with some sort of effect that was foreign to him. They looked as if they'd seen decades instead of days. Antique fixtures, paintings, and bartending equipment lined the shelves and other places.

It appeared as if his dream pub had been plucked straight from his mind. Francis had outdone himself, though the decorator claimed to be waiting for one or two final pieces for it to be finished. Haddy's would likely be open for business within a week or two.

Caddock felt a shiver of doubt at the idea. He still needed to hire his staff, including a chef. The pub couldn't run itself.

Loud voices drew his attention from thoughts of how to proceed with his plans. Caddock stalked over to the large stained-glass windows in the front of the bar in time to see Francis and a rumpled man in conversation. The stranger stumbled, wavering on his feet, making him seem drunk, and Francis took the chance to duck around him.

Before Caddock could say a word in greeting, Francis seemed to fall apart at the seams. His body shook while his breathing grew increasingly erratic. He sank to his knees while Caddock remained unobserved, watching him in growing concern.

Sherlock moved up to Francis, who was clearly in the midst of some sort of breakdown. He muttered something that sounded like a mantra to himself repeatedly. Caddock wondered if Sherlock had some therapy training from how the dog behaved.

He wished Rupert hadn't evaded his questions. There were clearly things about the decorator that he didn't know.

The realtor had gone out of his way to avoid responding to his calls.

Caddock crossed the room quietly and cautiously crouched in front of Francis. He had no experience with panic attacks. "Francis? How can I help you? Do you need anything?"

"Oh. God." Francis flushed a lovely pink that only made him more attractive. Sherlock scrambled into his owner's lap. Slender, trembling hands threaded into the sheltie's fur. "I apologize for my—"

"No, don't." Caddock cut him off, reaching instinctively to squeeze the man's shoulder gently. "What helps? Would you prefer I sod off and leave you alone?"

Francis's eyebrows lowered as he frowned at him in confusion. "Help? Me?"

Caddock wondered if he was still struggling to return to his calm self. Sitting on the floor, he leaned against a chair and waited Francis out. Their hands lightly touched with their thighs separated by barely a breath.

Long minutes passed in silence before Sherlock started to perk up. The sheltie bounced around, licking both of their hands and faces. It didn't take long for his boisterousness to bring out the hint of a smile on Francis's face.

The smile apparently signalled the end of the breakdown. Sherlock raced off to attempt to inspect the bag with his biscuits. It left Caddock with an obviously embarrassed and suddenly shy Francis.

"You blush." Caddock swiped a rough, calloused thumb across the flushed cheek, then smirked when the fair skin turned a deeper shade of pink. He got to his feet then yanked

Francis up as well. "Do you want to talk about it?"

"No." Francis stumbled slightly to sidestep around a table to avoid him. He ran his fingers through his out-of-control mop of hair. "Sorry. Patty is the village drunk. He brings up some rather dreadful memories for me. His breath alone can trigger a panic attack. I usually try to have them in private."

"Is Sherlock a therapy dog?"

"Yes." Francis glanced up then dashed over to rescue the bag of baked goods from the inquisitive dog. "He's a troublesome creature, but he helps. I'd be a miserable wreck of a man without him."

Caddock had stirrings of another sort within him. There had always been hints of dominance in his relationships. He enjoyed being the one relied upon and had struggled to find someone who would allow him to care for them. He found Francis almost unbearably enticing.

Ordering himself to behave, Caddock spoke casually about the work remaining on the bar. He offered Francis one of the custard tarts while tossing a peanut butter biscuit to Sherlock. The two eyed him suspiciously while he leaned against one of the support pillars in the bar with his own pastry in hand.

Fragile.

It was one of the words that struck him whenever Francis was near. Not that Caddock believed him to be weak. There was an immense amount of strength in the man, but fragility as well.

He'd been avoiding Francis for this precise reason. The fire of desire in his belly ignited further each time. He couldn't afford to want him.

They were all wrong for each other. Caddock was an overgrown brute of a man, older and experienced. Francis likely preferred someone more refined, and certainly younger.

"Caddock?"

*But, oh, the things that voice makes me want to do.*

He blinked a few times, trying to clear the haze from his sudden desire to drag breathy, pleasurable moans from Francis. "Something wrong?"

"Well, not wrong, but you've smashed a custard tart in your hand." Francis gave him a cheeky smile. "Did it need to be punished for being a naughty tart?"

"Naughty tart?" Caddock coughed on the bit of pastry he'd just taken. His eyes darkened at the bemused innocent grin sent his way. "Tarts often need a firm hand. I'm sure Stevie is familiar with it."

Francis gaped at him before collapsing into fits of laughter. He bent over at his waist, clinging to a chair for support. "I'll *never* be able to look Ruth in the eye again, not without giggling like a loon."

They shared a laugh while Caddock wiped the remnants of the custard from his fingers. He hesitated on the last one. Making a quick decision, his eyes stayed on Francis while he slowly and rather obscenely licked his thumb clean.

"I would—should—maybe." Francis spun around, walking straight into a table. "Must finish up here."

Caddock watched, completely amused while the man stumbled around, studiously avoiding him. "Can I help?"

"No, no."

"You certain?"

"Yes." Francis muttered "'Oh, God" under his breath, though Caddock heard him in the quiet of the pub. "It's all under control."

*Maybe there is hope after all.*

# Chapter Nine

"Oh, God, drown me in the sea." Francis sat in Watson, staring at the open door of the pub where Caddock was struggling with a large box. "And now he's bending over. Look at that arse."

Sherlock simply blinked at him, clearly unimpressed by the fine specimen before them. He also seemed anxious to get out of the Fiat. Francis wanted to take a few moments to compose himself.

It didn't help when Caddock seemed to take his time standing up straight. Finally, he did, pausing to stretch slowly. And *that* visual would be going straight into Francis's fantasies.

Dragging his gaze away from the immensely attractive man, Francis lectured himself sternly on avoiding doing anything even remotely humiliating. Running into furniture didn't evoke a sense of confidence in anyone. Cool and calm was required.

Cool.

And calm.

So of course, the moment Francis strolled casually into the pub, Sherlock cut in front of him. They stumbled over each other while he tried to avoid stomping on his menace of a dog. The move finally sent him hurtling towards the hard edge of the nearby wooden bar.

Strong hands caught him by the arms and lifted him up on his feet. Francis's eyes met Caddock's. He cursed his fair skin for blushing at their sudden closeness.

Francis cursed other parts of his body when they also reacted to the scent of Caddock. It was all male, a heady, complex combination of all the little things that meant Caddock. He found himself wanting to wallow in it.

And in Caddock, with his lovely muscled rugby body. Francis found his hands gripping those strong arms shamelessly. The Brute peered down at him with his lips quirked up slightly in amusement; neither appeared in a hurry to release the other.

"Morning." Caddock's gruff whisper sent a warm tingling down Francis's spine. He tugged Francis against his body tightly for a moment before finally releasing him. "I brought an extra coffee for you."

Francis thought several double shots of espresso wouldn't

be enough to shake him out of this stupor. This pub job needed to be over. It was hell on his emotions, never mind the rest of him.

"You've done brilliant work." Caddock gestured with his cup around the bar. "Can't thank you enough."

And another blush.

*Cursed genetics.*

Distracted by his frustrating skin, Francis failed to realize Caddock had moved closer. He started in surprise when a hand plucked the cup out of his hand. It returned to capture his chin to tilt his head up.

"I plan on kissing you." Caddock towered over him by a few inches. His eyes glinted with what could only be desire. "Now would be the time to punch me for being such a forward bastard."

"I might resort to violence if you don't kiss me." Francis hadn't enjoyed a decent snog in ages.

He felt dwarfed by the brute who wound his arms around him. His expectations were for a power kiss to match the man. Caddock drew him in with a teasing brush of their lips together. His tongue then teased Francis's lower lip. The light kiss had Francis searching for more. He opened his mouth and then Caddock struck with a practiced ease.

His arms were iron bands around Francis. Caddock's lips and tongue took control of the kiss. He explored every inch of Francis's mouth with a sensually dominant possessiveness.

"Better than coffee?" Caddock asked after tugging on his bottom lip with his teeth. Caddock's voice had dropped even lower which sent lovely shivers along Francis's spine. He'd never had a voice fetish before now. "I'm certainly awake."

The tight hold on Francis's chin didn't lessen at all. The Brute certainly preferred being in some semblance of control. Francis flicked his tongue against Caddock's lips, hoping for another snog or ten.

"Looking for more?"

Afraid his body would simply slump to the floor, Francis caught the sides of Caddock's striped rugby shirt. *Does he ever wear anything other than jeans and T-shirts of one form or another?* The arm around his back pressed in more tightly. It caused the hardening in his trousers to grind into the man's hard thigh.

"Devlin's off with his grandparents for the weekend." Caddock gained a firm grip on Francis with his fingers in his hair, dragging his head back. "I'll cook supper."

"For yourself?"

"And you."

"Are you asking me out?"

"In, actually." Caddock chuckled. "Say yes."

*Smart arse.*

Francis could frankly come up with a thousand reasons to say no, most of them involving some iteration of dating a client being bad for business. If it went horribly, the two of them would be stuck in a small village. Looe was filled with gossips. His gran was the chief amongst them.

He had a suspicious feeling the entire village would know about this dinner within hours of it happening. *Saints help me.* Was it worth all this for one date and some snogs? The confident smirk being sent his way took all his arguments and threw them in the rubbish.

"Yes." Francis took a moment to realize it had actually been his voice agreeing to dinner. "I'd love to have dinner with you."

Caddock's hands finally shifted away from him, tracing the seam of Francis's lips one last time before stepping back. "Good."

*Good?*

As if they hadn't been snogging five seconds before, Caddock disappeared up the stairs that led to the office above the pub. He caught a glimpse of the impressive bulge in the man's jeans. *Blimey.* It left Francis standing in the middle of the room for several minutes attempting to regain a semblance of composure.

Sherlock danced around him, trying to get his attention. The dog finally caught the sleeve of his cardigan in his teeth to drag his owner forward. He stopped when they reached the counter where the biscuits were sitting.

*Spoilt-rotten mutt.*

"Here, you overly indulged creature." Francis tossed one into the air, laughing when Sherlock leapt up to catch it. "Good boy."

*How the hell am I supposed to focus on the last details of the bar with a hard-on the size of the Thames in my trousers?*

# Chapter Ten

CADDOCK

Supper.

It seemed simple. And it was with a four-year-old. Francis might not be impressed by toast soldiers with thick slices of cheddar cheese and a healthy dollop of beans, but Devlin loved them.

The cottage seemed awfully quiet without Devlin in it. Caddock had turned on the telly in the den and the radio in the kitchen in the hopes it would fill the emptiness. He had enough nerves to deal with about the date without adding worry over his nephew to it.

# After the Scrum

Devlin *would* be fine with his grandparents. They had promised to talk each night and to read a chapter of *The Wind in the Willows* over the phone. It had become a tradition between the two of them.

Putting his nephew out of his mind for the moment, Caddock returned his attention to the organized chaos in his kitchen, only to find his attempt at pastry had turned into crumbly gravel. Maybe beef Wellington had been too much of a stretch. It had seemed easy enough in the video tutorial his chef mate had emailed to him.

Francis might not notice beans on toast, right?

*Get a bloody grip on yourself. You're the Brute. You don't cave in the face of a first date.*

He tossed the remnants of what had been dinner into the rubbish. It was time for Plan B, since Plan A had gone so spectacularly. Five minutes staring into his open refrigerator told him one important thing—living with a child had ruined his ability to be romantic on the spur of the moment. The clock in the den sounded, informing him there was less than an hour to get his shite together.

Plan B.

He scrubbed his fingers through his short, greyish-brown hair. Any trips to local restaurants would set tongues wagging, something to be avoided this early on. Gawking would certainly ruin any sort of romantic endeavour, yet another reason to stay at the cottage where they had guaranteed privacy.

Searching his mind for an idea, Caddock remembered a meal one of his teammates used to make frequently. The dish had become a tradition before all their big tournaments.

Rugby players could be a superstitious bunch of bastards.

A simple pasta bake with lots of cheese, spinach and chicken. It would be delicious, though not fancy. But then again, why be something he wasn't? It would be better to enter this—whatever it might become—solely as himself.

With the pasta in the oven, Caddock put together a quick chocolate mousse pie. It would set in the refrigerator while they ate. He could think of a number of things to do with the leftover chocolate so the bowl went into the cooler as well. Might as well keep it *just* in case.

Thoughts of Francis stretched out on his bed with a healthy dollop of chocolate mousse on his body flooded Caddock's mind. Getting himself so worked up before the date was a terrible idea. It was time to focus his attention on getting ready.

His hopes for the evening weren't overly grand. The two men had chemistry, explosively so if those kisses earlier had been any sign. Supper would hopefully expand on their tentative start.

And wouldn't it be nice to *not* be alone anymore? The majority of his retired rugby mates were all married with kids running around. He had the kid, maybe not the ideal way, but still, now he wanted a partner to share the madness with.

Caddock wandered over to the pull-up bar set up in one of the taller doorframes along the hallway. A quick set of chin-ups settled the uneasiness in his belly. He would sweep Francis off his feet.

It couldn't be harder than a tackle. He'd done it often enough on the rugby pitch. This would be less violent, and a hell of a lot more fun.

# After the Scrum

With twenty minutes left, Caddock had a quick shower. Not a vain man by any means, he still carefully selected jeans and a polo shirt that were ever so slightly tighter than necessary. Maybe Francis would stare at his arse again; it had been amusing to watch him in the reflection in the pub windows.

A knock on the door sent a surge of adrenaline through him. He sent a wicked grin at his reflection. It was time to see how many blushes he would earn this evening.

"Sherlock. *Stop it.*" Francis sounded more than a little frazzled on the other side of the door. The plea was followed by a thud and what sounded like glass breaking. "Please? We're trying to make a good impression. *No.* We don't eat the nice flowers. Mud isn't attractive. Naughty Sherlock, naughty. Wait until Gran sees us both covered in mud. I should've left you at home."

Holding back his urge to roar with laughter, Caddock opened the door trying to show concern and *not* amusement. Francis was frantically attempting to extract his dog from acquainting himself with the flower bushes that lined the outside of the cottage. Francis had dressed to impress, even wearing an intricately knotted cravat with his cardigan and jacket, but Sherlock in his exuberance had dragged the both of them through the mud.

They were *covered* in mud, flowers, and twigs.

It shouldn't have turned Caddock on at all. Yet, it did. A lot. He allowed the briefest moment of daydreaming about rolling around starkers in the mud with Francis.

*Sodding hard-on.*

"Need a hand?" Caddock returned his attention to his floundering date.

"Several." Francis blew out his breath in a rush, knocking loose a stray petal from his face. He gestured to a bag on the ground. "That *was* a bottle of wine. Sherlock apparently disapproved."

"But you don't drink, or *like* alcohol at all."

Francis shrugged, still struggling to untangle his dog from the garden. "I do on special occasions, sometimes. Regardless, you do."

Caddock shook his head sharply then reached down to lift Sherlock out of the bushes. He ignored the sharp branches that scraped his hands. "It makes you uncomfortable, so I can play teetotaller."

Gobsmacked was probably the perfect word to describe the look on Francis's face. Caddock didn't mind restricting his occasional beer or glass of wine if it would make the man comfortable. Panic attacks weren't conducive to a romantic evening.

No wine with supper seemed a small price for the opportunity to peel the layers of the intricately complex man. Lonely nights had taught him life was too short to waste a chance at a good thing. And Francis? He was definitely one of those.

With a tight but gentle grip on Sherlock, Caddock caught Francis by the arm to lift him up as well, helping him out of the slick mud, left over from the rain. They left the wine on the pavement for now—it could go in the rubbish later. There were bigger issues to tackle.

# After the Scrum

"He's a disaster." Francis stood on the rug inside the house. He stared dismally at the mud, which covered not only his dog, but his own clothes and the rest of him. "I'm a right mess myself."

"How about you have a nice hot shower while I give your Sherlock a quick bath?" Caddock had a cheeky thought and broke into a grin. "Or, better yet, how about we let the mutt have the shower, and I give *you* a bath?"

Francis seemed stunned into silence, his eyes glazing over with what Caddock hoped was desire. "Yes, er... no... I don't think Sherlock is safe alone in a bathroom. He might redecorate."

"I sense a story behind your certainty." He kept a gentle but firm hold on the sheltie while leading them further into the house. He ignored Francis's worried remarks about tracking mud all over. "Take the bath in my room, just down the hall, the second door on the right. I'll get this one situated then bring you something to wear. We can toss your trousers and everything into the wash while we eat."

Giving Sherlock a rather quick rinse and dry, Caddock returned to his bedroom to find a clean outfit for his guest to borrow. He had a feeling Francis might drown in his clothes, considering his much broader frame. Maybe he'd go starkers?

The thought brought back a reminder of the chocolate mousse and how delicious it would be. Caddock took a breath to reel in his out-of-control desire. *Naughty Brute, deliciously naughty.* It was too soon to indulge in wicked depravity.

He'd have to continue to remind himself it was only the first date. They had *plenty* of time for all those indulgent fantasies.

63

He turned it into a mantra when Francis stepped out with only a towel around his waist, hair dripping and face flushed from the warmth.

"I didn't have anything to change into." Francis gripped the towel tightly, eyes averted. "Can I borrow something?"

Caddock traced a drop of water travelling down Francis's chest with his gaze, hypnotized by the urge to lick it off. His voice came out much deeper than normal and slightly strained when he spoke. "I put them in the wash. My trousers would be too large, but I've got some shorts with a drawstring, and a T-shirt for you."

He grabbed the clothes and set them on the bed. They stood awkwardly for a moment. Neither of them wanted to acknowledge the naked truth between them, not yet.

Reaching out to scrape a blunt thumbnail across one of Francis's nipples, Caddock winked at him then left the room. Better to let him change in private. They'd never make it to supper otherwise.

*Too soon.*

He returned to the kitchen to start dishing out the pasta. A sheepish Francis joined him barefoot a moment later. Barefoot. In Caddock's shirt. He had to turn around and close his eyes for a second.

*You are not actually a brute. You can be romantic. Oh, and stop bloody talking to yourself.*

"Caddock?"

"Pasta?" He shoved a bowl into Francis's hands. "Thought we could eat in the den, maybe watch a film?"

*Or skip it all and snog.*

# After the Scrum

As Sherlock made himself at home on the rug in front of the fireplace, Caddock settled on his cosy leather couch. He turned slightly so his leg pressed up against Francis's when he joined him. Rough denim against bare skin.

*Oh, sod it.*

Setting both of their bowls on the nearby coffee table, Caddock shifted forward towards his date. He caged Francis in against the side of the sofa. Supper could wait; it was a taste of something completely different he was in the mood for.

Their lips had *only just* touched when a wet nose bumped him in the cheek. They turned to find Sherlock sitting by the couch, tongue lolling and tail wagging. He inched forward when the men attempted to continue kissing.

"Pasta and a movie it is." Caddock sat up slowly, easing Francis back up, letting his hands wander for a quick feel of the man's slender, but lithe body. "Next time, maybe leave your babysitter at home."

# Chapter Eleven

"Ruth told me she heard it from her Stevie who heard it from the milkman who heard Janice at the butcher talking to old Mrs Covington." His gran's eyes twinkled dangerously while she served up breakfast to him the morning after his first date. She pulled his marmalade out of reach. "Something you want to share with your dear old grandmother then?"

"No." Francis snuck a piece of bacon for Sherlock, who sat under the table. He smiled sweetly at her narrowed eyes. "So what *exactly* did Ruth tell you?"

The rumours had apparently run rampant through the village. Francis had been seen going into a *certain* someone's cottage. One person even claimed they'd been naked in the front garden.

"*Gran.*"

"I put no stock in you being naked—my Francis wouldn't be so obscene." She finally handed over the marmalade to him. "Did you enjoy yourself with your rugby star?"

"*Gran!*" Francis turned a shade close to the strawberry jam on her toast. He grimaced at the thought of berries. They were tart and disgusting things. "He's not *my* anything."

"Yet."

*Yet.*

"Please, Gran, it's new. We've barely… done anything worthy of gossip." He clung to his cup of tea, hoping for a hint of sanity. "I *like* him."

"You haven't *liked* anyone since that idiot Trevor." Gran's aged hand reached out to cover his. "Is he good to you?"

"We've only had one date."

"But is he good to you?" she insisted, still holding on to his hand.

"I think he might be."

The wheels were definitely turning in her mind, but surprisingly, she left the conversation there. Sherlock nudged his hand for another slice of bacon. They *both* received disapproving humphs from her.

Not wanting to draw out the morning, or give her a reason to start in on the grand inquisition, Francis rushed through his breakfast and left promptly. Watson, as always, provided a refuge for him. He'd delayed his antique hunt while working on the pub which left him behind on his work for several clients.

There was absolutely no reason whatsoever to stop by the pub to see if Caddock wanted to go with him. The man had a business to get started. It wasn't likely he'd want to traipse around the countryside watching Francis exclaim over every antique he stumbled across.

Even his gran tired of hearing him wax poetic about the differences between seventeenth-and eighteenth-century side tables. Why would a man like Caddock even consider it? Yet, it was a massive part of Francis's life.

Watson seemed to have a mind of his own. The Fiat was parked outside of Haddy's before Francis could even register making the right turns. It would just be a quick visit—nothing more.

No snogging. No tripping over things. And most definitely no staring at any portion of his anatomy.

"Ready for another movie?" Caddock sat at one of the tables surrounded by stacks of papers. He had a laptop in the centre of all the relatively organized chaos. "Been trying to get all my duckies in a row for the opening next week. Got the chef and a couple of bartenders lined up. Want a coffee?"

"I would ordinarily love one, but I'm on my way out of town." Francis shoved his hands into the pockets of his tweed jacket to keep himself from fidgeting. "I'm driving to Ardingly in West Sussex for their antiques fair. I won't be gone long. I didn't want you to think I'd faded into oblivion."

*And now I sound like a romantically constipated idiot.*

"Want company?" Caddock made a show of carefully gathering up all his papers and shutting down his computer, giving Francis time to close his mouth and hide his surprise. "I think I can squash into your Fiat. Or, if you like, we can take my Range Rover. It's not as friendly as Watson, but less likely to break my back."

"You want to go? You'll be bored…."

"I'll be with you." Caddock stood slowly, and Francis lost his battle with avoiding staring at him. He received a knowing smile in return for his perusal. "And Sherlock. Life isn't dull with the two of you around. Might want to avoid mud puddles, though."

"I'm confident you aren't nearly as hilarious as you believe yourself to be." Francis sniffed derisively, though the smile on his face refused to dim. "We can travel in yours. Though Sherlock's bound to leave hair on *everything*."

"I have a four-year-old, Francis. My vehicle has seen much worse than the hair of a shedding sheltie." Caddock stuffed all his papers into a leather case. "Follow me to the cottage? Watson can have a long car nap in my garage. I'll need to throw a travel case together."

"What about Devlin?"

"Still at his grandparents'." He gripped Francis by the shoulder to guide him towards the door. "Our first holiday and we've barely snogged."

"*Idiot.*" Francis elbowed him in the side and immediately regretted it. He rubbed his elbow with a pained groan. "Are you made of bricks?"

Caddock lifted up the hem of his sweater to reveal his contoured abdomen, so muscled it could've been carved out of stone. "Not quite bricks, though I'm hard-headed enough to be."

Something was definitely hard, and it wasn't Caddock's head.

The short drive up to the cottage left him no time to cool his thoughts. How on earth were they going to survive several days together if the sight of a stomach sent his libido into overdrive? They'd end up arrested for indecent exposure at some point.

Not something his gran would approve of at all.

It took a surprisingly short amount of time for Caddock to pack for the trip and lock up his home. Francis likely shouldn't have been surprised. As a rugby player, the man had spent a fair amount of his career flying all around the word.

Twenty minutes later, the two sat in the much larger Range Rover in awkward silence, still parked by the curb. They looked everywhere but at each other. Sherlock had already made himself at home on a pile of blankets in the back seat.

"All right, sod this, we're getting this out of the way now."

It was the only warning Francis received before Caddock had a hand in his hair, dragging him into a kiss. He held him there until they'd gotten their fill of each other—for now. Released back to his seat, he could only blink repeatedly, trying to settle his breathing while Caddock started the vehicle.

Francis shook his head when he caught Ruth on a nearby pavement giving him the thumbs up. "It'll be around the village in an hour, but they'll be telling everyone we were starkers."

"I could rip your shirt off," Caddock offered helpfully with a hint of a leer. "Could be a great way to pass the time, staring at you."

"Stare at the road," Francis snapped at him, annoyed at the

flush of colour that moved up his neck and cheeks. A strong, warm hand gripped his thigh and *stayed* there. It was going to be a long bloody drive. "Focus on the road."

"I can multitask."

# Chapter Twelve

CADDOCK

At times in his life, Caddock had experienced something his brother had called a paradigm shift. He'd always claimed to be too daft to have an epiphany. Haddy had said he'd just had his head rammed into the ground too many times.

With Francis dozed off in the seat beside him and Sherlock snuffling in the back seat, likely dreaming about chasing bunnies, it gave him a glimpse at what life as a married man would be like. And didn't that kick him in the arse. He wished Devlin was with them, if only to complete the picture.

*Too soon.*

*Far too soon.*

He kept his eyes focused on the winding roads, enjoying the sea breeze through the barely-cracked window. Driving had always been an escape for him. The paps and fans couldn't harass him through tinted windows.

It had become a sanctuary in the height of his career. In his early days, he could admit to having been an irresponsible fool. His lessons had been learned the hard way.

The tabloid covers that had graced the store shelves for weeks had been enough to straighten him up. It had also taught him to be more cautious about who was allowed into his life. His brother would've said he'd become *too* careful.

Not for the first time, Caddock found the ache left by his brother's absence almost unbearable. He started out of his darkening thoughts when a hand slid over his. Francis twined their fingers together.

"I've caught on to your evil plan." Caddock decided to lighten his mood. "You wanted a chauffeur for this four-hour drive."

"And someone to ogle." Francis nodded sleepily. "I'm a devious, nefarious sort of man."

Devious and nefarious were far from the adjectives Caddock would use to describe the man beside him. If anything, they might describe him. His father would certainly think he was corrupting the much younger Francis.

*Stanfords have standards.*

It was practically the family motto. Drummed into their minds from an early age, it hadn't been strictly followed by anyone in their family. His mother might be the exception to the rule.

"You shouldn't think so hard. You're more brawn than brain." Francis yawned then stretched languorously in the front seat, mildly impeded by the seat belt. He leaned forward to look at a passing road sign. "We're about ten minutes out. Want to stop for tea?"

"And a piss. I'm dying here."

"How very charming." Francis grimaced.

"What? It's been three and a half hours. Do you know how many cups of coffee I had this morning? I'd be knackered without them, but I'm drowning." Caddock pulled into a service station. "You grab the tea then?"

A miniature turquoise Fiat sat on the driver seat waiting for him when he returned to the vehicle. His passenger, already situated, calmly sipped his tea with a bland expression on his face. Such a silly thing, it touched him for some strange reason.

They drove the last little bit in relative silence. Sherlock had apparently declared nap time over. The dog raced from one side of the vehicle to the other, peering out the windows to bark at anyone they passed.

Francis picked at the edge of the paper cup holding his tea, clearing his throat nervously. "About the antiques… I feel I should explain or warn you."

Caddock spared a quick glance over when he fell silent, completely intrigued by the bizarre turn of conversation. What in the world could require a warning about shopping? "Yes?"

"It's only fair to warn you that I am prone to fits of occasional and acute obsessive insanity around them." Francis continued staring at his cup, missing Caddock's struggle to avoid laughing. "Gran says I become entranced when I'm near anything older than the nineteenth century. It's the nicest description she has for it. She's also accused me of being a nutter on occasion."

Caddock tried.

It took a valiant effort in his opinion to hold it in, but eventually the laughter refused to be contained. He roared with it, eventually having to pulling into the nearest parking spot, which luckily turned out to be the one set up for the fair. Tears streamed down his face while he tried to compose himself.

"So happy to have amused you." Francis struggled to release the belt buckle, fumbling with it. He appeared to think the laughter had been solely at his expense, or even worse, perhaps meant maliciously. "Blasted belt."

Caddock leaned across the armrest to capture the frantic fingers with his own. He waited until Francis finally looked his way. "I wasn't laughing at you. Well, maybe a tad. I promise, however, that I'm looking forward to seeing this insanity for myself."

"Idiot."

"I'm the brawn, remember?" Caddock caught Francis by the neck to yank him forward until their lips met. It didn't take long before he was biting and tugging on his bottom lip, sucking lightly to ease the sting from his forceful kiss. "You're showing me your world. I'm pleased. So stop overthinking every bloody thing."

With the emotional tripe out of the way, Caddock dragged his Francis into another kiss. He had to force himself to pull back when their hands started to stray under their shirts. The local bobbies wouldn't take too kindly to public nudity.

"The ancient artefacts await." Caddock allowed a moment to enjoy the bruised lips and mussed-up hair on Francis. He looked rather brilliantly debauched. "I haven't snogged in a parked car in years. Feels all nostalgic."

"All right, old timer. Why don't you hobble along with me over to see the other antiques? I'm sure they've missed you." Francis's laugh turned into a moan when Caddock snuck a hand out to, not so gently, pinch his nipple through his shirt. "Unhand me, you uncouth villain."

"Your moan doesn't quite match your words." Caddock easily blocked the attempted swat to his ribs. "Careful, don't want to hurt yourself again."

The good-natured teasing continued all the way to the grounds where the tents for the antique fair were set up. Their laughter drew some attention, but not as much as Sherlock. The rambunctious dog was remarkably well behaved, though.

A quick show of his therapy dog licence allowed them free rein without interference. Sherlock still managed to turn heads. It wasn't helped by the harness Francis had placed on him, identifying him as a service dog. It did prevent people from wandering up and petting him without permission.

Extreme obsession didn't begin to describe Francis once in his beloved world of antiquities. It seemed as if he lost himself entirely, drifting from tent to tent. Everyone else around him became nothing more than a distraction.

It fascinated Caddock to watch him. He'd never seen anyone so incredibly focused on discovery, with an intensity he hadn't seen since his rugby days. A strange sense of honour filled him at being invited to be part of this obviously important pastime.

Two hours into their search, Francis seemed to come back to himself. His sheepish grin did interesting things to Caddock. And most of those revolved around wanting to find a dark corner for a bit of privacy.

*Later.*

*I can debauch him later.*

Controlling himself became increasingly difficult the more time he spent around Francis. He was endearing in a way no other man had ever been to him. It was definitely time for him to up the level of romantic persuasion.

While Francis had been off in antique land, Caddock had made plans of his own. Several phone calls and a bit of name dropping had two side-by-side accommodations booked at the Gravetye Manor. The rooms shared a bathroom, and most importantly—a door.

Many hopes hung on that connecting door. Snogging served many wonderful purposes. It would be nice, however, to progress a little further.

While Francis drifted over to another area, Caddock drifted into a lurid daydream. His fingers itched to explore pale, toned skin. Francis might not be as workout driven as he was, but all the running around after Sherlock had definitely given him a supple physique.

Sliding one of his hands into Francis's pocket, Caddock let two of his fingers stroke the slowly growing shaft. He felt it when the other man wilted against him. His soft groan was thankfully almost inaudible.

"Someone's having some exquisitely wicked thoughts." Francis attempted to squeeze by him to get a closer look at a nearby gilded mirror. His arse grazed against Caddock, allowing him to feel the evidence of his earlier fantasizing. "What *were* you thinking about?"

He caught the decorator by the hips and held him in place. He pointedly ground his hard shaft against Francis. "You. All the bloody time, I think about what I want to do with you."

"Oh?"

Another subtle movement lined their bodies up perfectly.

"*Oh.*" Francis jolted forward when footsteps sounded nearby. He twisted around to adjust his trousers, much to Caddock's amusement. His chuckle earned him an annoyed glare. "You twistedly perverse old man."

"And you're enjoying every second of it." He smirked when Francis's eyes drifted down to the evident arousal in his jeans. "Wanna give me a hand with this?"

Francis blinked at him once and then a second time. "Tempting, but not when the lace is watching."

*Lace?*

A cursory glance around allowed him to spot the slightly off-colour lace curtains draped across several nearby shelves. There wasn't much else to do but chuckle at the absurdity of the moment. At the least, it was clear they were *both* feeling the high level of attraction.

Caddock reached down to scratch Sherlock's ear. "Your owner has me all tied up in knots."

"Just in knots?" Francis leaned around a tall grandfather

clock to smile at him.

"And many, many other things."

# Chapter Thirteen

FRANCIS

The door mocked him.

It sat on its innocuous hinges ridiculing him for all his inadequacies. The bland beige door held the secrets to the universe on the other side. Well, maybe not the universe. It definitely hid his next great sensual escapade.

Antique shopping had been fruitful. Supper had been delicious. The hotel was lovely.

It had been a surprise when Caddock pulled them up in front of Gravetye Manor. A luxury hotel in a sixteenth-century estate house in West Sussex, it was a place Francis had drooled over numerous times. He could never quite justify the expense of renting a room for a few nights during the annual antique fair.

And all Francis found himself doing was staring at one spot in the room. How utterly ridiculous. He wasn't some naïve virgin, even if he often blushed like one.

His granddad, a veteran of war, had always told him to face the hard things in life with his back straight and his chin up. Though sex probably hadn't been what he had in mind. Feigned confidence was still at least an attempt at it.

*All right. Back straight, chin up, knock on the door.*

Francis found his hand frozen an inch from the wood. *Don't be a cowardly custard, knock.* There was a ridiculous sense of relief when his knuckles finally connected. A rush of anticipation replaced the fear while he waited for a response.

A silly urge to hide behind a nearby chair struck him. He ignored it. Grown adults could indulge in all sorts of things behind closed doors. His desire to partake wasn't cause for embarrassment.

Even if some of his current wishes were a little out of his usual realm of interest. He had the distinct feeling Caddock would be more than up for the challenge. *Pun not actually intended.*

Caddock answered after a few moments, wearing a pair of grey boxer briefs and a grin. "You're overdressed for the party."

Francis didn't think silk pyjama bottoms equated to a full outfit. Sherlock ducked by the two men to make himself comfortable in front of a roaring fireplace at the side of the room. "Way to wait for an invite."

A brief silence followed before Caddock caught him by

the arm to drag him inside the room. It had a similar layout to his own, though the décor differed slightly. It was hard not to inspect every piece of furniture and ornamentation. The designer in him wanted to map everything out in his mind for future inspiration.

"I'm having a small nightcap." Caddock held a small glass of what appeared to be brandy. "I thought it might be nice to relax after a day of indulging your obsession."

Francis sank into one of the plush armchairs situated by the fire. He had to laugh when Caddock dragged the other one until it was next to his before taking a seat. "Rearranging the furniture? Isn't that my job?"

"I wanted to be close enough to touch." His hand slid easily across Francis's silk-covered thigh. He massaged the lean muscles underneath his fingers before making a show of setting both of their half-empty glasses aside. "Maybe more than touch."

Once situated in his chair, Caddock threw his arm out to catch Francis by the waist, dragging him over so he straddled Caddock. One muscled arm wound around his back for support while they paused, face-to-face with eager anticipation in both their eyes.

Spreading his legs so his knees rested on the chair instead of digging into his brute's thighs, Francis found the position almost immediately that pressed their groins together. Deep simultaneous moans resulted from the contact. A hand slid down his back to slip into the top of his pyjamas; calloused fingertips grazed teasingly along the crease of his arse.

Slight pressure from the hand inched him forward, which

in turn forced their shafts alongside each other, only separated by his silk pyjamas and Caddock's thin shorts. Francis rested one hand on the man's broad shoulders to steady himself. His other played absently with the scruffy five o'clock shadow on his jaw before leaning in to brush their lips together.

Intercourse could wait. It would have to wait, since he wasn't fully ready for it. The pleasure of a shared orgasm, however, had waited long enough.

The conversation regarding the progression of their budding relationship would come later. All Francis wanted to think about were the fingers teasing ever lower and the tongue insistently exploring his mouth. Then there was the glorious sensation of grinding against one other.

"Like it?" Caddock moved his fingers in lazy circles, still drifting further down. Francis's entire body reacted to the deep rumble of the Brute's voice. "Oh, yes, I think I could talk you into ruining those pyjamas, couldn't I? Have you dreamed about this? I've had some ruddy filthy ones about you—about all the inventive ways I want to fuck you and all the wonderful things I could do with this lithe body of yours."

"Saints above." Francis had trouble remembering how to breathe while all his senses were under assault.

The fingers delved further down his crease until they found their target at last, teasing his most sensitive area with light, fleeting strokes. Caddock kept his lips pressed against Francis's ear, whispering a stream of sensual filth. It all had his arousal rising.

His body moved of its own accord. He writhed in Caddock's lap. *What a glorious sensation.* Their shafts lined up perfectly and they quickly established a gliding rhythm.

Using his hand on Francis's arse as a guide and motivator, Caddock had him bucking wildly against him. It hadn't ever felt quite so overpowering. Francis couldn't ever recall being carried off into such a practically out-of-body experience.

The wicked whispered promises that caressed his ear would've likely been sufficient to bring him to completion. They assaulted his senses in a cerebral fashion, something no one else had ever bothered to do.

Caddock seemed to pluck all of Francis's most hidden desires from his mind. It drove him to rock wildly in his lap, their shafts hot and hard, rubbing together constantly—the silk and cotton fabrics covering them already more than damp with the evidence of their actions.

"I'm going...." Francis gasped for air, unable to complete his sentence. He tried again, but found it impossible to formulate the words.

"*No.* Not yet." Caddock nipped at his earlobe while shallowly thrusting the tip of his finger into Francis. It did nothing to ease the pressure for him; neither did his next words. "You'll wait until I say."

"Can't."

"You can." Caddock growled against his neck, biting then sucking the skin to leave a mark. "You want to be good for me, don't you?"

"Oh, hell." Francis thought he'd been electrocuted. Those words sent a charge that seemed to flow through every part of his body. These were deep fantasies he'd never been able to voice to anyone—never mind actually exploring them. "I need… have to…."

He was painfully aroused. Every shift of their bodies brought him closer to the point of no return. He wanted release so badly it hurt.

"Please."

"Would you like me to let you come?" Caddock's eyes darkened considerably. He hadn't stopped the miniscule movements of his invading finger, ever-present to drive Francis wild with want. "Would you? Ask nicely."

*What is he doing to me?*

"Please. Caddock. God, please. I must…." Francis trembled with the effort it took to *not* go off like a bottle rocket. He craved the added layer of the dominant game they were playing. It had been the one thing lacking from his previous encounters. "Please?"

Caddock pressed his finger in ever so slightly further. His smile widened at the sound it elicited from Francis, who writhed desperately above him. "*Now.*"

Everything faded into a strangled moan of pure pleasure. Francis's vision went white and the sound cut off, strangled by the raw desire in him. He practically erupted with the intensity of his completion.

By the time Francis regained some semblance of awareness, he found himself naked on the bed, with Caddock using a wet flannel to wipe him clean. Words didn't come to him until after they were cuddled under the comforter with Sherlock hopping up to curl at their feet. Even then, he didn't quite know how to verbally express how good it had been for him, not without over-inflating Caddock's ego. It was something the man certainly didn't need any help with. The smug grin on his face was bright enough to be blinding.

*I have to say something.*

"Nice."

*Smooth, Francis, real smooth. Apples are nice. Beans on toast are nice. Incredibly hot, sweaty sex?*

"More than fucking nice." Caddock started to roll over just as Francis lifted up. Their heads connected with an impressively painful thud. Caddock flopped down on the mattress, clutching his face. "Somewhat less fucking nice now."

Francis collapsed on his back, gently prodding the already growing goose egg on his forehead. "You've concussed me."

Caddock snorted in amusement while leaning over to tenderly check out the injury. "I'm sure I can find inventive ways to wake you up to ensure you aren't going to die in your sleep."

"How kind."

# Chapter Fourteen

Three in the morning was way too damn early to be awake. Caddock couldn't seem to drift back off though with so many thoughts filling his mind. He had so many questions that had yet to be answered.

Francis had seemed receptive to his particular brand of pleasure. People often tended to say all sorts of things in the heat of the moment. Better to confirm it when they weren't drunk on pleasure.

It had been a long time since he had been able to let go with another man. His own enjoyment in many ways had derived directly from causing his partner to lose control in such a powerful manner. It was intoxicating.

Thinking about their earlier pleasure drew his attention back to the naked body flush against his own. Shaking his head, he used the breathing exercises from his rugby training to focus his mind elsewhere. It wouldn't do for Francis to believe he had sex permanently on the brain—even if it was the truth.

Flexing his arms, Caddock shifted the man in his arms slightly. Brown hair brushed against his nose, tickling his nostrils. He tried valiantly not to sneeze.

He really did.

Pinching the bridges of his nose, Caddock tried to will it away. Nothing worked. He finally twisted his head around sharply to sneeze loudly, the sound barely muffled by his pillow.

The sound reverberated around the quiet room like a blast from a canon. Sherlock shot to his paws, barking wildly and searching for the intruder. Francis also sat up, though a little more slowly, looking adorably befuddled.

"Arm the battlements." Francis blinked owlishly in the dimly lit room, the bump on his forehead standing out more than it had earlier. "Arm the… what?"

"Arm the battlements?" Caddock stared at his young lover, confused and amused. "You been watching period war movies or something?"

Francis yawned, stretched, and then finally turned half-open blue eyes towards him. "My granddad's favourite exclamation, left over from his days in the military no doubt. It stuck in my mind. So why did the Brute roar in the night?"

Ignoring the now quietly growling Sherlock, Caddock

seized Francis by the leg to shift him once again into his arms. He then rolled them so they were side by side. Not being alone in bed was something he could definitely get used to enjoying.

"Sleep, cub." Caddock began to run his fingers through Francis's chaotic mess of brown hair. He tugged lightly on the strands before stroking. "Sleep."

"Cub?" Francis tried to sit up, sounding mildly indignant. He stopped, and then glanced over his shoulder. "I think I gave you two black eyes."

"Me. Brute." Caddock smirked at Francis who was clearly struggling to stay awake even though he continued to glare at him. "You. Cub. And yes, you did catch me right between the eyes with your pointy head."

"We'll discuss your inventive ideas of nicknames and the circumference of my head after I've slept and consumed copious amounts of coffee and...." Francis trailed off into a slurred mumble, which was followed seconds later by the start of a barely audible snore.

They woke several hours later to the sound of the concierge ringing with their courtesy wake-up call. Francis hadn't wanted to miss the earliest part of the last day of the fair. It took a minute or two to untangle themselves from the mess of limbs, complicated slightly by the enthusiastic Sherlock trying to greet them with liberal licks to their faces and wags of his tail.

Dog breath at seven in the morning did not constitute a pleasant wake-up. Sherlock, it seemed, had been anxiously waiting for his morning walk. He grabbed his leash and dropped it on Francis's head, directly on his bump.

"Ow." Francis winced with a pained groan. "Has anyone ever told you that you have an exceptionally hard head?"

"Something's hard." Caddock thrust his hips forward to brush the truth of his words against Francis. "How's your bump?"

"Sore." Francis slipped out of the bed and blushed practically from head to toe at his nudity. He rushed into his own room with Sherlock hot on his heels. "I'll… see you downstairs."

Caddock chuckled for a moment then hefted himself out of bed with a heavy sigh. It seemed last night hadn't completely relaxed Francis. *Good.* He quite enjoyed being the reason behind that flushed skin.

Knowing they had an hour before Francis would become impatient to leave, he jumped into their shared shower. It might be fun to provide a bit of a visual temptation if he was walked in on.

The connecting door never opened though. Caddock finished up and dressed in a fresh set of jeans and one of his old training jerseys. He sat in the lobby of the hotel, reading a paper with a cup of coffee, waiting for Francis to join him.

It gave him ample opportunity to allow his mind to consider the risks he was taking. Anyone who had the media's attention had to work incredibly carefully to watch their image. He'd never given a rat's arse about sharing most aspects of his life, but this was different.

He'd never been truly active in the *community* as such. The London scene could be a bit much for him. And he'd never met anyone like Francis there.

Or maybe he hadn't really been looking all that hard.

"Careful, you might strain something with all those lofty thoughts." The man occupying his thoughts swanned by, stealing his cup of coffee then heading towards the front door with Sherlock at his heels. "Coming with?"

Shaking his head in amusement, Caddock followed the two out of the hotel—after obtaining a second cup of coffee. Punishment could be meted out for the loss of his original cup. It'd be amusing to see how many fantasies they shared.

He spoke first with the hotel concierge about having supper delivered to his room. No way would they be sleeping separately again on this short trip. One night had given him a taste of the joys of having Francis in his life—and bed.

With his orders placed for the evening, Caddock headed out of the hotel to hunt down his companions. Sherlock and Francis appeared to be playing a game of tag around his Range Rover. Francis ran by with his dog nipping at his heels, stopping only once he was completely out of breath.

"Enjoying yourself?" He grinned at them, watching Sherlock, who sat panting at their feet with his tail wagging happily. "I'd pay several quid to bottle his energy."

"Sherlock felt the need to express his displeasure at being cooped up all night." Francis pulled a portable water dish out of his satchel and set it down for the thirsty dog. "I had to soothe the savage brute before taking him around delicate artefacts."

Caddock raised his eyebrows then glared between sheltie and Francis. "Savage brute?"

"You two have a lot in common." He retrieved the bowl,

opening the rear door of the vehicle to let Sherlock hop inside. He turned a suspicious frown towards Caddock. "You are remarkably calm about your stolen coffee."

He waited until Francis had started past him to the passenger side of the vehicle to grab him by the arse and yank him closer. "I'll exact payment eventually."

Francis coughed several times, turning his head to the side to attempt to hide the flush on his cheeks. "I look forward to your attempts. And to laughing at your failures."

"You cheeky bastard." He squeezed his arse one last time then shoved him towards the other side of the Rover. "Hop in, cub. Time to get your old furniture fix."

"You make me sound like I'm addicted to furniture polish and dust."

"The first step to finding help is admitting you have a problem." Caddock reached over to help when Francis struggled with his seat belt—again. "How do you ever drive your Fiat if you can't even work a buckle?"

"My Watson adores me. He'd never impede my ability to drive with finicky issues like this nonsense." Francis's eyebrows lowered in obvious aggravation at having to be buckled in. "I've decided to name your vehicle Dr Evil—over the top, flashy, and prone to bouts of wickedness."

"Really? Dr Evil?"

"Suitable name for a recalcitrant vehicle owned by a brute." He glared petulantly at the seatbelt then focused his attention on the passing scenery. "It hates me."

"And yet, Dr Evil has managed to safely cart your precious antiques around without complaint." Caddock always found it highly amusing the way Francis talked as if cars were living, thinking beings. "Perhaps he should demand a few quid in compensation for being overwhelmed by dust and mould?"

"You're a rather lippy chauffeur." Francis retrieved a treat from one of the front pockets of his bag and tossed it over his shoulder to the excited Sherlock. "Attractive, but mouthy."

"You didn't seem to mind my mouth last night. You begged for more, cub." Caddock sipped his coffee then focused on driving.

As they spent more time together, he found they fell into an easy, playful companionship. His sense of humour differed slightly, yet still complemented Francis's own. They laughed—frequently. It had been one of the pieces missing from his previous relationships.

By the time they pulled into the parking area once again, coffees had been finished. Francis placed the therapy animal harness on Sherlock and they set off for the tents they'd missed the previous day.

Since it would be another morning and afternoon spent meandering amongst the antiques, Caddock was content to let Francis inspect each item. He, on the other hand, mentally plotted out the rest of his plans for the evening. It didn't have to be perfect, but special.

Frotting with the man had been spontaneous—enjoyable certainly, but not a true representation of what it could be. Tonight would be different. He hoped.

Sherlock brushed past him with a wag of his tail, which brought to mind a potential issue. Perhaps a massive beef bone to distract the dog should be the first item on his to-do list. It would be a bit of a mood killer to have him putting his wet nose in the middle of an intimate moment.

Maybe a sedative? No, bad idea, Francis would strangle him with a necktie for even thinking about it. And Caddock had far more interesting ideas for what to do with the numerous ties the man owned.

The visual of Francis nude with nothing but a necktie on caused an uncomfortable tightening in his jeans. He compounded it by suddenly thinking about tying the man up to his bed with them. Suddenly, the rather harmless scrap of silk fabric took on a life of its own.

# Chapter Fifteen

By the end of the fair, Francis had managed to pack the back of Dr Evil—the Range Rover—to capacity. A satisfying trip, but that was mostly owed to the company. Antiques could be found any time, after all.

He had never shared a trip quite like this with anyone—outside of his gran. Rupert did occasionally take him places, but only to review properties in need of his decorative touch. Neither held the overtly romantic hints this had.

The hotel itself had been quite a step up. He was being wined and dined. Seduced. And honestly, he couldn't even begin to find it in him to resist.

Why would he? Francis *wanted* Caddock. At a deep level,

he craved everything about him. Resisting would be pointless and counterproductive.

The only worrying part of the day had been the almost constant contemplative look on Caddock's face. Plotting. The man had something up his sleeve. And *that* thought shouldn't have been nearly as arousing as it was.

Despite all their joking around, Francis knew Caddock had more than simply brawn going for him. A keen mind hid beneath all the muscles, and not one to be underestimated either. It made him want to get to know the man even better.

After spending hours touching dust-covered things, a bath had been his first priority when they arrived back at the hotel. Well, second actually. Sherlock had required a long walk, food, and a good brushing before settling down. Only then did Francis allow himself to enjoy the luxurious bathroom, sinking into the warm, bubbly water.

"Are you decent?" Caddock tapped lightly on the door.

"No."

"Perfect." Caddock entered, holding two long-stemmed glasses filled with what appeared to be champagne. "Drink?"

"What *are* you up to?" Francis accepted the glass while sinking lower into the water. The soapy bubbles covered his important bits. His less-than-subtle move earned him a bark of laughter from his intruder. He racked his mind for a safe— and non-nudity involving—topic of conversation. "Is supper ready?"

"Not quite." Caddock eased down to sit on the floor, his body squashed between the wall and the tub. "Got something you can eat in the meantime."

# After the Scrum

"*Prat*." He noticed after a while that his normally ever-present dog was nowhere to be seen. "Did you lock Sherlock in the wardrobe?"

"Me?" Caddock's grin had *nothing* innocent about it. "Concierge found a large beef bone available at the butcher's. The little menace will be occupied for hours."

"Hours?"

"No cold noses where they shouldn't be." His blue eyes no longer held laughter, but something darker and deeper. He leaned forward on his knees, arms resting on the edge of the tub so they were practically nose-to-nose. "I've got a *number* of ideas for how to fill the time before we eat."

"Any of them legal?"

"Three out of five."

Caddock's arm slid into the water with hardly a splash. He trailed a finger across the top of Francis's knee. A slight pressure from the digit had him letting his legs fall apart, pressed against the smooth sides of the tub, allowing the hand to dip further down.

"Not so long ago, this would *definitely* have been illegal." Francis strived for casual. No need to let on how incredibly affected he was by the rough, calloused skin grazing over him under the water. "I'm in the bath to get clean, Caddock, not dirty."

"Oh, we'll get you clean. I'm flexible enough to do both." His hand moved firmly and steadily to stroke Francis. It took an embarrassingly short amount of time for him to be on the brink. Caddock gave him a wicked grin. "You're going to finish now, cub. Then I'll get you nice and fucking clean."

97

The command in Caddock's voice brought him there almost instantly. The things the man did to him. It was like being a teenager, but without the pimples, copious Byron quotes, and questionable clothing choices.

True to his word, the water was emptied then the tub refilled. The last time someone had bathed Francis, he was fairly certain he'd been a child. This experience felt entirely different and incredibly intimate.

It was sweet and obnoxious. Caddock particularly made a point to find every spot on his body that was even the slightest bit ticklish. He ended up dunked under the water when he sent a wave of suds at the man washing him.

They went into an all-out water fight. A massive tip would definitely have to be left for the housekeepers. The bathroom looked like a storm had blown through and left bubble bath *everywhere.*

Caddock attempted to lift him out of the water only to slip in the suds, releasing him, on the now slick marble. He crashed onto his back with a painful-sounding thud. He grabbed Francis on the way down, causing him to bounce on his chest.

"Fancy meeting you here." Francis eased up. "You didn't break anything important, did you?"

"Too hard-headed to break my skull."

"I said anything *important.*" He got to his feet then held his hand out to help Caddock. Instead of lifting him up, he ended up on the floor for a second time. "Not the best idea I've ever had."

A familiar sound of nails on the slick floor told Francis

that they'd drawn Sherlock's attention away from his bone. He sniffed both men then skittered out of the room. The sheltie had never been overly fond of baths.

"Something we said?" Caddock grabbed a large plush towel to wrap around Francis's frame. He, of course, took a moment to arrange the fabric, fingers teasing the spent body now partly shielded from view. "Ready for supper?"

"Pardon?" Francis blinked at him, shaking the wet hair out of his face. He'd lost himself for a moment. "Will you *stop* doing that so I can think clearly?"

Caddock flicked one of his nipples lightly then stepped away with his hands up. "I'll stop, but I can't promise you'll be thinking clearly."

Leaving aside the obvious truth of how much the man affected him, Francis grabbed a second towel to dry his hair. The water dripping into his face was driving him up the wall. It allowed him to at least try to appear suave.

The sound of the door chime pulled Caddock away to deal with room service's delivery of their meal. It gave Francis a chance to not only dry himself off, but dress and attempt to tamp down his arousal. He shouldn't be raring to go so soon.

Once Francis had determined Sherlock was still happy, curled up on a massive dog bed near the fire in his hotel room, continuing to gnaw away at his monstrously large treat, he made his way through to find Caddock chatting with the young woman who'd brought up their meal. She offered a smile to him before leaving with an empty tray under her arm.

If pressed the next day, Francis wouldn't have been able to remember exactly what they'd eaten. The brute sitting beside him worked endlessly to arouse him. From the innocently light accidental touches, to firm squeezes every once in a while, and the constant press of their thighs together, he was left with a heightened sense of awareness—never mind the permanent state of hardness.

Those thick fingers of Caddock's shouldn't have been capable of such deft, nimble touches. The meal was over before he even recalled having taken a bite of anything. The empty plate was his only proof that he'd eaten.

He'd thought they would move immediately towards the bedroom, with clothes flying.

He'd been right.

*Partially.*

Dessert had been next. It would *definitely* be something remembered for years to come. In fact, Francis wouldn't ever be able to look at chocolate fondue the same way again. It had seemed so unremarkable in the small, heated bowl.

The gleam in Caddock's eyes told another story. It might not have been the bedroom, but clothes definitely disappeared remarkably quickly. Francis thought it all went by in a blur.

So much so, it took a moment for him to register what had happened. With a practiced ease, Caddock had the table cleared and a naked Francis spread across it. The bowl of chocolate rested innocently in his hand.

"Might be a tad warm." Caddock held a spoon up high, allowing the liquid chocolate to drizzle in a curved line down the centre of his abdomen. Francis hissed at the sudden heat only to moan when Caddock began to lick up the sweetness. Caddock smiled. "Relax, cub, I've barely gotten started."

*Easy for him to say.*

Francis had never been adventurous sexually, at least, not outside of his vivid imagination. The molten chocolate dripped over sensitive parts of his body sent pleasurable shivers through him. Warm enough to excite, but not to hurt. He had no doubts this had been planned carefully.

One finger dipped into the bowl then brushed against his barely parted lips. Francis opened his mouth further, letting his tongue flick against the bittersweet chocolate. He sucked on the digit, giving a fine demonstration of what he'd do to other parts of Caddock when offered the chance.

"Still hungry, cub?" Caddock took a mouthful of the chocolate then replaced his finger with his tongue.

The chocolate-flavoured kiss was brief and tasty. Francis wanted off the table, but his wrists were grabbed and his arms lifted over his head. A stern glare told him to hold them there.

*Interesting.*

What followed was a slow torture of bites, licks, and teasing ticklish touches. He had no idea how the man had learned all of his secretly sensitive parts in such a short time. It felt like they'd known each other for years rather than the short time they had.

By the time the dish had been emptied of its liquid contents, both men were liberally covered in drying chocolate. The table and rug underneath it had splotches of it as well. He didn't want to even think about what the hotel staff would wonder when they saw the mess.

*A problem for another day.*

Lifting him up from the table, the Brute hefted Francis

over his shoulder to carry him into the bath. His protests at being carted around like baggage were completely ignored. *Not surprising.* He glared at Caddock after being deposited in the standing shower that was attached to the tub.

"I'm having the strangest sense of déjà vu." Francis blinked then yelped in surprise when cold water suddenly hit his back. "*Caddock Stanford.*"

Caddock blinked at him in surprise. "You sounded remarkably like my mother just then. Don't do that. It's disturbing."

"Prat." Francis found himself pressed up against the cool tile of the shower. The water hitting his body slowly went from icy to a more comfortable warmth that began etching away at the sticky mess plastered to his body. "Haven't you tired yourself out of bathing me?"

Caddock pressed up against Francis's back, his hard shaft finding a comfortable home against his arse. "Not about the fucking bath, cub."

"Oh?" He flicked warm water into the Brute's face. "You have to admit it does appear to be about cleanliness at the very least. Doesn't it?"

And then a finger dragged down his spine to delve where Caddock's impressive length had rested a moment earlier. Francis found it impossible to stop his body from responding. He pushed against the welcome intruder, wanting to feel more—feel deeper.

"*My cub.*"

Francis's stomach tightened at the possessive growl. He sternly reminded himself swooning was *not* attractive or manly. Better to infuse a note of caution before Caddock carried them both away.

"Little early for using 'my', isn't it?" Francis impressed himself with his steadiness of his voice. He hadn't thought himself capable of stringing a sentence together at this point. "You have a lot to prove before I consider you worthy of the right to claim me as anything."

"I better get started then." Caddock twisted his finger around, eliciting a moan from Francis. "I don't think it'll take long."

# Chapter Sixteen

CADDOCK

"Uncle Boo. *Uncle Boo.*" Devlin raced up the walk to launch himself at his beloved guardian. He giggled when he was swung up high into the air. "Again, again. Do it again."

Caddock hugged the lad tightly then tossed him high over his head, easily catching him on the way down. They both waved to his father (and Devlin's grandfather), who drove off without a word—strange. "Did you have fun this weekend?"

"Gwannie and Gwandad made toast soldiers." The little boy leaned in closer to whisper in his ear. "Yours taste better. Oh. I saw bunches of sheep. And Gwandad said a naughty word."

He found himself stunned into silence. He could count

on one hand the number of times his father had sworn in his presence. "Did he really? Did your granny wash his mouth out with soap?"

"Ew, Uncle Boo." Devlin wrinkled his nose. He threw his arms around his neck while they headed into the cottage. "He said... he said... I don't 'member. Oh, I do. What's a poof, Uncle Boo?"

He almost dropped his nephew at the innocent, but emotionally loaded question. "Poof? Is that the naughty word Granddad said?"

"Gwandad said, 'no son of mine is a poof.' And Gwannie whacked him on the head with a spoon." Devlin seemed to find that bit particularly funny. "Then they went in the garden to talk all quiet so I wouldn't hear."

Sitting with his nephew in his lap in one of the comfortable leather armchairs in the den, Caddock explained some men liked other men instead of women. He carefully tried to avoid disparaging the lad's grandfather, but didn't hesitate to mention "poof" was a hurtful word. It was a word he should *never* use.

Devlin frowned seriously up at him, fingers fidgeting with the button on his jacket. "How come Gwandad was being a meanie? He called you a naughty name."

"Me?"

"You like Fwannie." He reached into his pocket to pull out a photo clipped from a newspaper that showed Caddock, Francis, and Sherlock together in Sussex in one of the tents. "Gwannie let me keep it. Can I go with you next time? Pwease?"

That was it?

"Of course." Caddock frowned at the image. "Where'd you get this?"

"Gwannie cut it out for me from a paper." Devlin wiggled off his lap to run towards the kitchen. He raced back seconds later. "Can I have a bickie, please?"

"One," Caddock said firmly before the pout could start. "There's shepherd's pie at Maggie's restaurant. If we go for an early lunch, maybe we can get a slice before they run out." He chuckled when Devlin ran off to clamber up onto the counter to grab his chocolate biscuit. "Only *one*, little Devil."

With his nephew briefly occupied, Caddock moved to his laptop to check in with his solicitor. He wanted to know where the hell a tabloid had gotten a photo of him from this weekend. It had been a while since the paparazzi had followed him around.

Maybe a fan had seen him and snapped the shot then sold it?

His guess turned out to be correct. A fellow shopper had messaged a brother who worked for one of the larger tabloids. The photo had been impulsively taken, not a sign of him being followed around. With luck, the story would be buried without any further interest.

"Uncle Boo?"

He leaned around the corner, balancing on the back legs of the chair to find Devlin munching on one of his biscuits. "Yes?"

"How come Gwandad's such a meanie?" His little nephew had inherited his keen sense of honour and loyalty from his father. Haddy would face down anyone and anything for someone he loved—even family. He'd often gone off on their father about this exact same subject. "I wuv you, Uncle Boo."

"Love you, too." He got out of his chair and swung the lad up onto his shoulders. "No more biscuits before we eat. You'll spoil the shepherd's pie."

The young boy had a massive heart of gold. Caddock had worked hard to keep him out of the middle of the drama between him and his father over his sexuality. He didn't want to taint the bond between grandfather and grandchild with adult issues.

His father would be in for a surprise if he intended to try to put a wedge between uncle and nephew over this. Devlin adored him. He also had, even at his young age, a dislike for name-calling and meanies.

It was the main reason Caddock had gone out of his way to be absent for the lad's visits with his grandparents. It worked, most of the time. Bloody tabloids. He knew a long, arduous conversation with his father would have to happen soon.

*Damn.*

Haddy's will had been specific on who had custody of Devlin. It went to Caddock. His lack of relationship had been part of why his parents, or more specifically his father, hadn't tried to fight him in court over it.

If the man knew about Francis, it might reopen that bloody issue again. He would have to send a second message to his solicitor. Better to have all the paperwork lined up and not need it, than be caught off guard by demands. Hopefully, his mother would be able to rein in her husband.

He didn't want their family torn apart even further. Devlin

had lost both of his parents. Any fight in the courts would only end up hurting him the most.

They were seated at Maggie's café, scoffing down their lunch, when it dawned on him. Francis had no idea about the tabloid article. And in a small village like Looe, all it would take was for one person to see it and *everyone* would know.

*Damn, damn, damn.*

He should've thought to call Francis immediately. His solicitor might be working on discovering if they had any legal action. It wouldn't help anything if it disrupted the man's life.

"You okay, Uncle Boo?" Devlin swung his legs in his chair, bumping the table every few seconds. He carefully separated his peas from his carrots, sticking his tongue out at the latter. "Ew."

"*Devlin.*"

"But Uncle Boo." He pouted, kicking the table leg until his uncle frowned at him. "'Kay, but only half."

"All right, my little negotiator." Caddock had to hide his smile behind his pint. It wouldn't do for the mischievous Devil to know he was amused. "Eat your peas and I'll let you visit Francis and Sherlock before we go back to the cottage."

Devlin eyed the peas like they might attack him. "'Kay. Pwomise?"

"Of course."

*Pick your battles, Caddock, pick your battles.*

# Chapter Seventeen

Francis

Gran had pounced on him the moment Francis stepped across the threshold into the kitchen from his bedroom. She flourished a paper in her hand, waving it wildly in front of his face. He closed his eyes to avoid the sudden onset of dizziness.

He gently caught her arm to stop the fluttering script and hopefully keep himself from the bout of seasickness. "What has you in such a tizzy?"

She smiled so widely at him it must've hurt, and also immediately put him on edge. "Someone said he'd only had *one* date. Someone told me to ignore all the rumours floating around the market."

"And?"

"Someone's in the *Daily Mail*." Gran opened to one of the back pages where a single photo of him with Caddock appeared. They were strolling with Sherlock at the fair, nothing damaging or suggestive about it. "Something to share with your dear old gran, love?"

"It wasn't…." Francis caved to the pleading clear in her cloudy eyes. He felt a slight stab of pain when he remembered how crystal clear her eyes had been when he was a child. "We had a weekend-long date. It went brilliantly. You'll love him, Gran. He's the antithesis of Trevor."

"I'll take a pan to his head if he hurts you." She moved over to start making tea. She nattered mostly to herself, but still managing to direct it to her grandson. "Invite him to supper tonight with his adorable little lad. Sweet wee boy. He's a good man to take in a young orphan. It can't be easy being a single father when you weren't expecting to be one."

Knowing it would be pointless to argue with her, Francis nodded his agreement. Caddock would *definitely* need a warning about his gran. Was anyone ever prepared for the great gran inquisition? Dodging her invitation to sit and chat over her fresh-made scones, Francis grabbed one on his way out the door. He opted to walk, mostly for Sherlock's benefit. The poor sheltie had been cooped up for hours.

They went the long way to his office, which left Sherlock more than ready for a long dog nap. Francis prepared to focus his attention on the new antiques purchased over the weekend. He had plans for some of them; others would need to be carefully stored away for future projects.

He made his way up the narrow stairs with his dog close

behind. They both stopped inside at the familiar blond sitting in his chair. "Rupert."

"So there I am, eating my eggs and sausage, as you do, when my beloved Joanne screeches like a banshee about a love connection." Rupert's green eyes were shrewd as always. He tossed a copy of the tabloid onto the nearby desk. "What *have* you been up to, young Francis? And how could you have kept it from me? I thought you cared."

"Easily. You gossip more than the entire village." Francis picked up the paper and swatted him on the head with it. He had to admit they made a handsome couple. "Did you come for the sole purpose of driving me to the brink of insanity? Or something more?"

"Mostly." Rupert picked a small airmail envelope out of his pocket then handed it over to him. "Graham's arriving tomorrow. Come for supper? Bring the Brute."

"*Rupert.*"

"Joanne will cry if you don't." Rupert clutched his hands to his chest, sinking to the floor on his knees. He crawled over to him, wailing dramatically. "Save me from my woman's tears, sweet lad."

"Get off the floor, you overacting prat. How your wife puts up with you, I have no idea." Francis dodged away from his friend's kick. "I will attend your repast and force myself to deal with your insufferable company. Joanne owes me a massive slice of her treacle tart for this."

"You secretly adore me."

"Like a pimple on my arse." Francis ignored the laughing buffoon and began organizing the first of the antiques. He

111

waited until Rupert had settled down to speak gain. "Will the tabloids cause trouble for Caddock?"

Rupert turned serious for the first time. "He'll rip them apart if they even think about harassing you."

"What am I doing? He is so far out of my league." Francis gave up pretending to catalogue his finds. He set the candlestick in his hand down and ran his fingers tiredly through his hair. His chest tightened painfully at the thought of letting Caddock go. "What *am* I doing?"

"Being a class-A moron?" Rupert strode across the cramped space to wrap his arm around Francis's shoulders. "Now all the shite you just said sounds far more like Trevor talking than you. I wish you'd let me and Graham handle the tosser."

He had a point, though Francis wouldn't tell him. The world would be a much better place if his ego were deflated ever so slightly. He had no doubts it wouldn't last.

"Go away." Francis glared at him. "Seriously, don't you have properties to sell and souls to damn to hell?"

"Now, now, no need to get testy because you know I'm right." Rupert let go of him and started for the door. "Our place, tomorrow at seven. Bring the Brute, Sherlock, and the little Devil. Oh, and I left a file on your desk for a new client."

"Prat."

Rupert left without responding. *Typical.* Supper with his gran this evening, then tomorrow with the Hodson family… it would be an interesting two days. It felt far too soon to have to deal with all of this.

Then there was the pink elephant in the room. Graham.

# After the Scrum

How would seeing his best mate after years go? They'd left on good terms, but distance hadn't helped them remain close.

Shaking off old memories, Francis wandered over to the boxes on the floor. He'd gone through two with five left to go when his thoughts were interrupted by a knock on the door. Five knocks, to be exact.

"*Fwannie!*"

An exuberant child bolted towards him when the door was opened. Only Caddock's hand shooting out to grab him kept Francis on his feet. He carefully lifted Devlin up into his arms.

He heard *all* about the peas and carrots—"ew gross"— eaten in order to see him. "Vegetables are good for you."

Devlin frowned at him with all the seriousness of youth. "Did you hitted your head, Fwannie? Sometimes Uncle Boo acts funny and says it's 'cause he hit his head."

"My head is perfectly fine." Francis smiled at the lad while trying not to glare at Caddock whose shoulders shook with his attempt to conceal his laughter. "You'll understand when you're older."

"Like with kissing?" Devlin looked up at them both with wide-eyed innocence. "Gwannie said so."

Both men choked slightly. They shared an amused smile. Between child and dog, there was certainly no shortage of entertainment.

"Yes, Devil, just like with kissing." His uncle reached over to ruffle his hair. He smiled ruefully at Francis. "Out of the mouth of babes?"

Warned not to knock over anything priceless, Devlin ran over to sit on the floor next to Sherlock. Caddock spotted the tabloid still on the desk where Rupert had left it. The man's eyebrows furrowed in obvious annoyance. It sent a sliver of doubt and worry into Francis's mind.

"Bastards."

Francis felt the tightness in his chest grow. He wiped his hands on his trousers a few times. What if Caddock thought it wasn't worth all the trouble? The man had clearly gone to great effort to avoid being in the press lately.

He wouldn't risk it for Francis. Why would he? Not with his nephew to worry about.

*Stop it. You are worth it.*

Caddock rested a heavy hand on his shoulder, guiding him out of the range of little ears. "I couldn't give a fuck about the idiots aside from them invading *our* privacy."

"Oh."

"And, cub?" Caddock cupped his chin and tilted his head up slightly. "I'm not going anywhere."

"Ever?" Francis always found it difficult to strive for collected when the Brute had a hand on him. "You might get a tad bored."

"Cheeky." He bent forward to press their lips together.

Quiet giggling drew their attention back over to Devlin, who appeared to have been whispering to Sherlock. The lad demanded biscuits on behalf of his friend—and himself. They nodded to each other; it seemed a trip to Ruth's was in order.

To their surprise, no one batted an eyelid at the little group while it walked through the village. Francis did catch several of his gran's friends sneaking photos, likely to share with her. He shook his head at the ridiculousness of it all.

# After the Scrum

The entire village had obviously decided to take a keen interest in them. It would've been endearing if it hadn't been so incredibly humiliating. Caddock, of course, chose to laugh about it.

Sherlock and Devlin had both been thrilled with all the attention. They happily trotted side by side, munching on biscuits Ruth had snuck to them. Did *everyone* around them have to be clinically insane?

"Can the ground swallow me whole now?" Francis asked after the fourth person had asked Caddock to sign the photo from the tabloid. "We are surrounded by nutters."

"Present company excluded or included?" Caddock asked curiously.

"Included."

# Chapter Eighteen

CADDOCK

If honest with himself, Caddock would admit to truly enjoying the way Francis turned so flustered around his grandmother. She was a sweet woman who went above and beyond to make him and Devlin feel comfortable. The meal hadn't been five-star, but it had been delicious.

She'd teased her grandson rather mercilessly. Francis had a permanent flush on his cheeks. Devlin had wanted to know why "Fwannie's all pink."

His laughter hadn't been appreciated, if the hard kick to his shins was any indication, but Caddock couldn't hold it back. He'd never experienced such a relaxed family supper in his life. He intended to enjoy it to the fullest.

# After the Scrum

The palpable love between grandmother and grandson shone through clearly. Caddock could easily imagine how being raised by this woman had shaped Francis. It had allowed him to flourish into who he was meant to be. Others might not have been quite so understanding of his eccentricities.

"Hurt my boy and I'll turn you into a Cornish pasty." She smiled sweetly at him, and then disappeared into the kitchen to prepare dessert.

"I've never been threatened by a grandmother," Caddock remarked absently.

A novel experience to be sure.

The rest of the evening went smoothly. Francis managed to avoid blushing quite so violently. Caddock thought it was a damn shame.

Devlin had been disappointed to be leaving. He'd pouted when Caddock said no to a sleepover, only cheering up when promised they'd have dinner again the next night, with Rupert. He wasn't looking forward to the chaos the blond could cause—and usually enjoyed causing. Being reunited with his twin would make it worse; the two might not look the same, but their personalities were damn near identical.

Having the prodigal brother, Graham, return had been an interesting turn of events. Francis seemed almost tense about it. Caddock had decided it wise to let the matter rest. They'd see tomorrow how things went.

With an audience of grandmother and nephew, they'd left each other *without* the snog Caddock really wanted. Devlin had been so worn out from playing with Sherlock, the lad had passed out asleep in his arms on the way to the cottage.

Once his nephew had been tucked into bed, Caddock sank into a chair by the fire in the den with a tumbler of Scotch in hand. He took a sip then lost himself in thought. It had been a good night; tomorrow might be slightly more difficult.

He slouched further into the leather cushions with a sigh, lifting his glass to no one in particular. He said with a wry smile, "Here's to old whiskey, younger men, and good food."

* * * *

The following night, Caddock volunteered to drive them to the Hodson house. Francis surprised him when he left his canine shadow at home. He claimed to want one less mischievous bugger to deal with for once.

A mate from his rugby days, Caddock knew Rupert could be a handful—age hadn't mellowed the man at all. He wasn't as familiar with his twin brother. Graham had already been overseas when they'd met. But from Francis's words, he would likely be exactly like his brother.

The evening would require patience and beer, not necessarily in equal doses either. His nephew could provide at least a partial shield for the madness. He had a particular talent for drawing attention to himself without even trying.

"Will Wupert let me play in the garden?" Devlin broke the silence in the vehicle. He swung his blue teddy around to hit the driver seat. "Hurry, Uncle Boo, Wupert might eat all the food."

Caddock barely heard his nephew's chattering. He worried more about the silent man seated beside him. Reaching over the centre console, he took Francis's hand in his own, resting both on the man's thigh. "Don't worry, little Devil, Joanne won't let her husband eat all the supper before we arrive."

Tension radiated off Francis. Caddock squeezed his hand gently. It wouldn't be wise to question him too deeply with little ears listening in on the conversation. Adult chats and issues would remain with the grown-ups. So Caddock offered support the only way possible in the enclosed vehicle: through touch. The tension eased slightly, but Francis still held himself like a goal-kicker about to make a match-winning attempt.

Once they arrived at the house, Devlin immediately raced inside. He'd been there numerous times. Rupert and Joanne were favourites of his, even babysitting him on occasion.

"What's got you so tightly wound?" Caddock caught Francis by the arms, stopping him on the front walk. He shifted his hands up to gently massage the man's shoulders. "Rupert's always sounded incredibly fond of you. I can't imagine him doing anything to cause this much anxiety."

Francis brought a hand up to scratch the side of his head. He took a second to then fix his hair. "I am aware of his character."

"So what's the issue?" He dragged his thumb along the side of Francis's neck. "They don't bite. I'm starting to worry about you. What is it?"

"History," Francis answered enigmatically. He ducked under Caddock's arm. "Not all memories are enjoyable to revisit."

"Don't worry your pretty head about it, cub. The Brute'll save you from the nasty idiots." He caught up to his lover only to be elbowed in the stomach. "What?"

"Worry my pretty little head?" Francis parroted back to

him with a frigid glare.

"Sorry." Caddock grinned completely unapologetically, and then crowded him into the house. Raucous laughter could be heard inside. "Maybe I'll hide behind you."

"Prat."

He was swatted on the arm this time.

"Oh, I do love seeing the Brute put in his place." Rupert's cheerful greeting drifted over from where he was tossing a happily shrieking Devlin back and forth across the room with Graham. "We found a rugby ball. He's a tad long and lumpy though."

"Wupert. Stop it." Devlin protested when he was shoved underneath the man's arm. "Bad Wupert. Put me down."

"Oh, it's Boo." Rupert set the lad down and grinned at Caddock before ducking the punch thrown his way. "Touchy, touchy."

"Play nicely, lads. I'll not be replacing any furniture. Are we clear?" Joanne stood in the doorway of the kitchen with her hands on her hips. Her dark green eyes flashed with amusement. "Behave or Devlin and I will eat the grand feast by ourselves, right?"

"Yes, JoJo." The little boy skipped away from the men to take her hand. "Can I help cook?"

"Of course."

Rupert exchanged a broad smile with Caddock. "He's four and he can already out-charm the lot of us. Sad, so immensely tragic."

The blond threw his arms out widely and gave Francis a dramatic, "Welcome to our humble abode." He apparently chose to ignore the fact that they'd all been to the house multiple times before. The man did have an annoying tendency to be rather theatrical.

As if to prove the report, Rupert bowed low with a flourish. He took his brother by the arm and forced him towards Francis. The two old friends stood awkwardly in front of each other—silent and uneasy.

"Oh for...." Rupert placed a hand on his brother's back and shoved him off balance. "Hug or something. Punch each other. Do something. I'm tired of moping letters from around the world about how 'Francis never talks to me.' And I'm sick of watching Francis stare mournfully at Graham's pictures. You're both blithering idiots, so you have that in common."

Graham punched his brother in the arm. "Shut it."

"What? You two were thick as thieves at university." He crossed his arms and glared at the two men before taking Caddock and guiding him out from behind Francis. He leaned in to whisper, "Let them sort this out themselves."

He'd have been happy to let them "sort it out." The trouble was neither man appeared to be capable of bridging the gap. They didn't really know what had started it. Silence stretched out between all of them, only broken by the occasional outburst from Devlin in the kitchen.

"I'm sorry." Francis broke the quiet, likely unable to handle the tension any longer. "You were right, and I am sorry."

Graham, a slightly taller and broader version of his brother, looked completely bewildered at his best mate's apology. "The hell are you on about? Did.... You can't possibly have thought I was pissed at you for Trevor?"

"Well then, what was it?" Francis stepped away from the man. His hands went into his cardigan pockets, likely balled into fists, something Caddock had noticed he did when stressed. "Was it all the travel?"

"Mostly." Graham closed the distance and yanked Francis into a hug. "I thought you had a crush. Didn't want you to be broken-hearted."

"Seriously?" Francis stepped away and then did something so out of character that both Caddock and Rupert gasped. He slammed his fist into Graham's jaw. "You egotistical prat. A crush? On you? I had absolutely zero interest in you."

"Sorry?" Graham rubbed his chin, letting his brother help him to his feet. "Can we strike it off as youthful arrogance?"

Caddock strode over to step between the men, staking his claim subtly and unnecessarily. "He prefers *older* men."

Francis shifted out from his embrace. "I will be in the kitchen with the only sane individuals in this madhouse."

"Something I said?"

# Chapter Nineteen

The kitchen turned out to be a brilliant refuge to gather his thoughts. Joanne plied him with extra bits from the trifle she'd been putting together for after supper. Devlin sat on the counter, munching on his own pieces of sponge cake. They all seemed rather happy to leave the idiots in the living room to argue amongst themselves.

*A crush?*

*A crush.*

It had never occurred to him. Rupert and Graham both had fallen almost immediately into the friend category—closer to brother, honestly. The more he thought about it, the more aggravated he became.

His time in London, after the attack and break-up with Trevor, had been rather chaotic, emotionally speaking. And then without warning, his closest friend had disappeared on him. It had seemed obvious to him at the time why.

Now, not so obvious.

"I'll set them straight, don't you worry." Joanne handed him a cup of tea then ordered him to keep an eye on the stove and the menace perched on the counter. She disappeared out of the kitchen before Francis could dissuade her. Her voice carried over to them, causing Devlin to giggle. "Wupert's in trouble."

"You blond twits! What did I tell you, Rupert? You're on the couch tonight."

Francis moved over to stir the sauce simmering in a pot. It smelled delicious even if he wasn't entirely certain what it was. She'd always been a brilliant cook, trained under one of the best chefs in London before they'd moved back to Cornwall.

"Fwannie?" Devlin held out a chunk of cake. "Don't be sad, Fwannie. Uncle Boo'll kiss it better. He's vewy good at it."

"Yes, he is." He smiled at the little boy. "Why don't we see if there's any extra custard in the bowl?"

"Hands *off* the custard," Joanne warned them both sternly. "I'll toss you both out on your ears."

"Not the ears." Francis grabbed a once again giggling Devlin and carried him swiftly out into the living room, where the three men appeared to be nursing their egos and glasses of whiskey. He set the boy down on the floor, pointing him

**124**

towards a play area with Legos that had obviously been set up for him, before turning his attention to the men. "She told you three then."

As if on cue, the two brothers fell to their knees. They shuffled forward to Francis, holding their hands out in supplication. He raised his eyebrows when they began to apologize in multiple languages—promising him everything from their first-born to gold and all number of ridiculous things.

*Idiots.*

"Get off the floor. Honestly, you haven't changed in all the years I've known the both of you." Francis found himself smothered in an embrace between the two men. He flailed his arms, trying to shove them away. "Would it be too much to ask for a bit of oxygen before I suffocate and am unable to accept your apologies?"

The rest of the evening went by rather smoothly. The five adults enjoyed lively conversation, interrupted periodically by Devlin. It had gone altogether more smoothly than Francis had imagined.

His anxiety over the evening proved to be completely pointless. With the apologies out of the way, Francis found himself sinking into the familiar camaraderie with Graham. They picked on Rupert ruthlessly, much to Caddock and Joanne's amusement.

After the meal, Devlin played quietly by himself, eventually curling up under a quilt to fall asleep. Joanne carried him upstairs to the guest room. She returned with a bottle of brandy to share.

Francis waved off the offer of a drink.

"Still?" Graham watched him in surprise. "I'd have thought you'd eventually bring yourself to enjoy at least a glass once in a while."

He shrugged, striving for indifference and falling short, if his friends' faces were anything to go by. "I don't begrudge anyone their enjoyment, and I do on the rare occasion."

"Francis."

Getting to his feet, Francis stepped out of the room, heading towards the back door into the garden. A small water feature in the back, dimly lit by faerie lights, offered a soothing oasis of sound for him. He closed his eyes, breathing in the crisp night air, letting it wash over him.

Strong arms wound around his body and tugged him into a firm chest. Caddock bent down to rest his chin on Francis's shoulder. He twisted his head to brush his lips against his neck.

"They mean well."

"I know."

And he did know. The brothers had done more for him than anyone outside of his grandparents. Their brand of exuberance could be a bit much for him—for anyone really.

Everyone had demons. Alcohol had been the trigger for his for years. Still was. Francis didn't think avoiding drinking himself should be that much of an issue.

It remained his choice. Graham's words had touched a sensitive spot for him. He knew it likely hadn't been meant as censure, yet it hurt nonetheless.

Time.

His therapists always said his anxiety would fade as years

went by. Yet, Francis, on his worst days, could still *feel* the fists hitting him. The only difference between then and now was the attacks happened less frequently.

He hadn't forgotten. Couldn't forget. And if not drinking helped, anyone with complaints could take a leap in the nearest river.

Francis would deal with this in his own way. Yes, Sherlock did most of the work. But he was still healing—continuing to progress forward.

*Doesn't it count for something?*

Caddock tightened his arms around Francis. "Fuck 'em."

"Blond is *not* my type." Francis couldn't help sinking into Caddock's warm embrace. "I'm growing quite fond of greyish-brown."

"Calling me old?"

Francis twisted around and gripped Caddock by the neck to tug him closer for a kiss. "Maybe not old, but in the general vicinity of it."

"Shut up." Caddock silenced him with a long kiss, grabbing him roughly by the arse to press him closer. "I *am* too fucking old for you."

"Only if the plumbing doesn't work." He couldn't help the cheeky retort even though it earned him a bite on his neck. "At least we know the teeth are still yours."

"Oi, no shagging in my garden or I'll hose you both down." Rupert stood grinning at the two of them through an open window. He cried out a second later when his wife grabbed him by the ear and dragged him away. "Oi, woman, let me go."

"He's sleeping on the floor tonight." Caddock sounded highly amused by this. "And you, cub, are sleeping in my bed."

Their quiet interlude under that cloudy night sky was interrupted by an ever so slightly subdued Rupert and Graham. Joanne appeared a moment later to abscond with Caddock into the house. It left Francis to stare uneasily at the two men.

"We're sorry." Graham gestured to his brother, *accidentally* smacking him on the chest. "For being, and I quote, 'childish idiots who don't have the sense God gave a mule.' Though, in our defence, mules aren't the dumbest of creatures."

"We are also, 'emotionally deprived buffoons who wouldn't grasp sensitivity without being bludgeoned by an anvil.' Did I get it right, love?" Rupert glanced over his shoulder at the still-glowering Joanne. He gave Francis a wink when he turned back around. "We forget, because it didn't happen to us, and I'm truly sorry for it."

Graham took a step forward, taking Francis by the shoulder. "I missed my best mate. I'm a blithering idiot, as your gran would say. Joanne had a right to rip us up for it."

"Apology accepted." He didn't see a point to not doing so. They'd likely grovel on the ground if he didn't.

Rupert's normally permanently cheerful smile disappeared. He moved up and rested a hand on Francis's other shoulder. "Accepted, but not forgotten? That's a good Cornwall lad. Your granddad would be proud of your obstinacy. He'd also have booted us in the arse. We've always thought of you as a younger brother."

Francis allowed them to squash him between them in a

hug—a very manly one complete with slapping each other on the backs. "You're going to leave bruises if you don't ease up. *Idiots.*"

Once Rupert left to convince Joanne things were back to normal, Graham took a seat on the garden bench and pulled out a cigarette. Francis declined the one offered to him. His old friend tilted his head to stare up at the obscured sky, pausing every once in a while to take a puff.

"I ran into Trevor in London last year." Graham flicked ash on the ground carelessly, though Joanne would likely murder him in his sleep for it later. "He's still a moody shit of a man. He asked about you so I broke his jaw."

"*Graham.*"

"He deserved it."

"You cannot go around breaking people's jaws." Francis rolled his eyes at the absurdity of it all. "Did he cry?"

"Sobbed like a wee child." Graham transferred his cigarette to his other hand then reached into his pocket to pull out a pocket watch. He held it up to Francis, who immediately recognized it as a Christmas gift from their second year of university. It hadn't had the indention on the front case though. "Saved my life."

"Good. Except you've ruined an antique." Francis frowned at the dented watch. "Honestly, can't you take care of anything? It's like year one at uni all over again."

"And you still nag like your gran." He clapped Francis on the thigh and grinned up at him. "I missed you."

"Then don't act like a prat again."

# Chapter Twenty

Despite his well-earned moniker of Brute, Caddock tended to be easy-going off the rugby pitch. His temper rarely, if ever, rose beyond being mildly annoyed. He'd always found life to be too short to allow anyone to get such a rise out of him. More often than not, his emotions stayed on an even keel.

Yet a single envelope from his mother had brought on a monumental amount of rage. It seemed his father had decided to speak with the family lawyer. He wanted to file for sole custody of Devlin.

The bastard wanted to take his Devil away from him. Caddock breathed out hard, clenching his fists and trying desperately to reel his anger back. It wouldn't do any good to punch walls or scream at the wind.

*Be calm.*

He would need a clear head to deal with all of this. No way would anyone take Devlin from him without a fight. Being named in the will as sole guardian would certainly help his cause.

The letter from his mother had also included some advice, which he was loath to actually take. She wanted him to allow them to have Devlin for a week. For two reasons: one, because it might help de-escalate things with his father, and two, the little Devil might be able, in his special way, to talk some sense into his granddad.

*No, I won't… can't lose him.*

"Uncle Boo?" Devlin tugged on his sleeve, his blue teddy bear dangling from his other hand. "Can we go see Lock and Fwannie?"

"Not right now." Caddock lifted the boy up into his arms, holding him on his hip. "How would you like to go see your grandmother and grandfather again?"

"But… how come? Gwandad was a meanie. Wanna stay here." Devlin's eyes filled with tears. "Don't wanna go."

Steeling himself for the onslaught of pouting, Caddock begin preparing the lad for a week away. He could see the wisdom in his mother's advice. It would leave him free to head to London to speak in person with his solicitor. Everything had to be carefully lined up to fight this.

Many, many tears were shed while Devlin tried to convince him not to take him to his grandparents' house. Caddock wondered briefly if the lad could sense his own inner turmoil.

He tried to keep it from him, but it wouldn't be difficult to tell how upset he was even if his nephew didn't know why exactly.

The quiet cottage hadn't seemed so devoid of life since they'd moved in to the place. Caddock sat at the table, letter in hand, staring at it dumbfounded. His brother would've been truly saddened by the demands his father wanted to make.

Haddy had been incredibly open to everyone. He wanted the same open-mindedness to be something his son learned. It had been part of his reasoning for granting Caddock custody, as opposed to their parents.

Sending a quick email to his attorney, Caddock made plans for a trip to London. It might be a wise idea to call in a few character references, just in case. He would have to speak with Francis before leaving though.

What a complete mess.

Nothing in life was more important to him than his nephew. *Nothing.* Every aspect of his life revolved around ensuring the lad's life was as perfect as possible without his own father. The trauma of a custody hearing could have far-reaching consequences for everyone. This had to be stopped before it progressed beyond a level they could control.

"Caddock?" Francis stood by his open driver side window, looking at him with concern evident in his eyes. "You've been out here for twenty minutes. Ruth called me to tell me she was worried you'd had a heart attack or something. What's wrong?"

He handed over the letter from his mother and got out of the Rover while Francis read it. "My father has gone completely nutters. If it wouldn't hurt my cause, I might go beat some sense into him."

"Would you really?" Francis didn't look up from his reading.

"No, but I'd think about it." Caddock might be furious with the man, but he was still his father. "I might take a piss in his garden."

"You are *not* taking a piss in anyone's garden, let alone your parents'." Francis finished his perusal of the letter while they got back in the vehicle to start on their way. "Where you going then?"

"London."

"I'm coming with."

"*Francis.*"

Francis crossed his arms and glared stubbornly at him. "I *am* going with you."

"Stubborn arse."

Francis remained strangely quiet for the first fifteen minutes of their drive. He fidgeted constantly as if struggling with himself. "Perhaps we should stop seeing—"

"*No.*"

"Caddock."

"I said fucking no." He would not sacrifice his best chance at a lifetime of happiness in a relationship. "We're not throwing the start of something brilliant for an ignorant arse like my father."

"But it might help you with custody. Devlin—"

"Devlin deserves an uncle at his best. I would *not* be at my best without you." Caddock yanked the wheel to the right and guided his vehicle to the side of the road. He twisted in his seat to make it easier to lean across until his lips were inches from Francis's, keeping one hand firmly gripping him by the shoulder. "Not giving you up when we've only touched the surface of how bloody amazing this could be."

Francis seemed momentarily flustered then shot forward to close the distance between their mouths for a kiss. He pulled back a little breathless moments later. "Well, if you're certain."

"I am."

As a rule, Caddock had spent a lifetime being the one others depended on for things. He had broad enough shoulders for it. No lovers had ever been so adamant about having his back in a tough situation. Most of the people in his life assumed he had a handle on everything.

The hand holding his while they drove into London meant the world to him. The freely given support had the surprising effect of choking him up. *Bloody emotions.* Now was not the time for it.

Three stops. Six coffees. Two trips to the loo.

Caddock hadn't been so wired on caffeine since his promotion to the national team. Mainlining coffee would be worth it if Devlin returned to him without too much of a fight. It would be a win if they could gather their small family back together instead of ripping it even further apart.

*Damn Father.*

*Damn him.*

His fingers flexed around his sixth cup of coffee. They currently sat in the swanky outer office of his solicitor—waiting. The limits of his patience were being tested in the extreme.

"Devlin isn't going anywhere. Try to stay calm." Francis

rubbed calming circles on Caddock's thigh with one hand while gently taking the cup from his hand before he crushed it. "Have faith."

"Faith in what?" He wouldn't put it past his father to pursue this as high as required to receive full custody.

Nodding absently at the comfort offered to him, Caddock returned his attention to his mobile. Texts had been sent out to one of his former managers, one who happened to be knighted, who had readily agreed to provide a reference to the courts if necessary. One of his mates had spoken with his parents, a duke and duchess, not bad people to have on his side.

"Caddock?" Francis tapped his hand several times. "You're about to break the chair."

He blinked then slowly unclenched his fingers from around the arm of the chair. *Shit.* "Sorry."

Francis waved off his apology. "Your Devil has been threatened. I wouldn't expect you to do anything other than fight for him."

Caddock gave the man at his side a half-hearted smile. "I'd fight for you as well."

A laugh and a roll of the eyes were the only responses Francis gave him to the declaration. It might've been ridiculous, but he meant the words. There weren't many men in the world like the one sitting beside him. Who wouldn't fight to keep him?

When called into the office, they found the solicitor had already put together quite an arsenal of defence. Caddock calmed slightly when he explained the difficulties anyone would face trying to disregard a legal last will and testament.

Parental wishes tended to supersede these sorts of conflicts.

They'd fight it.

And they'd win.

# Chapter Twenty-One

London had been a bore. Three days of meetings, mostly, had been worth it if only to thwart the plans to remove Devlin. Looe had been a welcome sight. Francis found the larger city only served to make him feel uneasy.

The downside to yet another multiple-day absence from Looe with Caddock had been the number of tongues wagging about them. Local gossips were worse than anything a tabloid could print. Everyone had opinions on the matter. It was exhausting to deal with.

Caddock had returned home to his empty cottage. Francis had disappeared into his office. The rumours could and likely would continue to swirl around the village.

"It'll all work out, love."

Those had been Gran's great pearls of wisdom. Utterly unhelpful. She trusted too much in the good in people. Francis had learned the hard way *not* to depend on it. Lowering expectations lessened the chance for undue pain.

He glanced down at the floor plan spread out on his work table. One of Rupert's new clients wanted their bedroom redone. For several hours, he'd sat trying to make progress. His inability to focus had begun to truly frustrate him.

Francis must've picked up and set down his mobile ten times in the last thirty minutes. The urge to check in on Caddock was almost compulsive. They could survive without seeing each other for a few days.

*Lovesick fool.*

He quickly shook the thought away. Not allowing himself to drift off into useless daydreams, Francis returned to the blueprints. *Honestly.* An eighteenth-century-inspired bedroom shouldn't be so difficult. His fingers flipped absently through wallpaper samples. He wanted it to have the right feel of underdone luxury.

Happy clients meant more business. Plus, one of the paintings he'd picked up at fair needed a home. It would fit in perfectly with the bedroom set he'd seen and flagged on a furniture list for a London auction house.

He tossed aside sample after sample, hunting for one to go with the particular shade of blue in the landscape watercolour. The shades were all beginning to blur in his mind. Decisions would never be made at this rate.

"Oh, this is beyond ridiculous." Francis tiredly scrubbed his face with his fingers. He huffed out short breaths, trying to wake himself up a bit. "You are completely capable of thinking about things other than a man for more than ten seconds. Pull yourself together."

It had been like this for days. Caddock had been busy—understandably so. And Francis had apparently turned into a swoony teenager in a romance novel.

*Idiotic. And ludicrous. Beyond it.*

*I wonder what Caddock's doing now?*

Francis dropped his head to the table, cushioned by the stacks of carpet, paint and wallpaper. "Hopeless, love-struck fool."

*Love?*

The thought had him on his feet so suddenly the chair crashed to the floor. Sherlock instantly shot up out of his bed, barking madly while searching for the intruder. He sneezed abruptly then sidled over to his owner looking decidedly confused.

"Sorry, Sherlock." Francis knelt down to give his dog a good scratch, deftly evading the wide tongue that tried to bathe his face. "How about a walk?"

Deciding they both needed some fresh air, Francis gathered up his work to leave it in some semblance of organization. He hated leaving his small workspace in a mess. It ensured he'd spend the rest of the day twitching with the urge to return to clean it.

He had to laugh at himself, remembering the time he'd gotten up at three in the morning to return to the office. It had been during one of his busiest weeks. But sleep wouldn't come until the space had been straightened up, so better to deal with it now than later.

With Sherlock on his heels, Francis headed outside and up the street. They meandered their way through tight streets on the way to one of their favourite parks near the outskirts of town. The longer walk would rid the sheltie of some of his exuberance and leave him ready for a nap upon returning for work.

Hopping over the stile with the dog close behind, Francis started for a nearby bench, content to let Sherlock run off his excess energy from being cooped up all morning. Instead of his usual manic circuits around the enclosed space looking for creatures to chase, he made a beeline towards a row of hedges along the east side.

Curiosity got the better of Francis when the dog stubbornly sat by the spot, unmoving and trying to get his attention with quiet barks. With an exhausted groan, he pushed himself off the bench. He began moving faster when Sherlock stopped barking and began to whine, something very out of character.

What had he found?

His heart stuttered briefly when blue eyes peered out at him through the thick hedge. *Saints above.* Francis would know those eyes anywhere. Thank God he'd decided to take a walk.

"Devlin, love, I'm going to help you out from there, all right?" Francis crouched in the grass, ignoring the thorns scratching his hands and arms. He made a space large enough for the four-year-old to safely crawl out without hurting himself. He fell on his back a moment later when the boy rocketed into his arms. "It's all right, love, don't cry. Sherlock's here. We'll keep you safe. He might even share a peanut butter biscuit with you. Can you tell me how you got here?"

"Fwannie." Devlin wrapped his short arms tightly around his neck while he sobbed against Francis's shoulder. "I don't wanna go to Gwandad's. I want my Uncle Boo. Can I go home now? Pwease?"

Francis couldn't help the tears in his own eyes at the boy's obvious torment. He held him close, letting Sherlock squash up close to sniff and lick at Devlin. They needed to contact someone. Distraught as the lad was, it probably paled in comparison to Caddock's panic if he knew his nephew had run away.

Shifting the boy in his arms, Francis retrieved his mobile from his pocket. He tried Caddock four times—receiving voicemail each time. Neither Rupert nor Graham answered their phones either.

*What now?*

They couldn't stay at the park indefinitely—not with the darkening skies warning of an impending storm. It was time to make their way home. He could drive over to Caddock's cottage to see if he was there.

And once Devlin had been settled safely, Francis would drive his gran over to pay a visit to Caddock's father. If anyone could strike fear into the heart of the man, it would be her. She terrified even the hardest sailors around Looe.

"Fwannie? Am I in twouble?" Devlin's fingers gripped his cardigan while he rested his head on Francis's shoulder.

He sniffled every so often while they walked. "Is Uncle Boo gonna be mad?"

Francis stopped as they reached where he'd left Watson parked earlier. "Your uncle loves you, Devlin. He'll be so happy to see you that I doubt he'll even remember you were a little naughty."

"Pwomise?"

"Without a doubt."

"What's a doubt?"

*Oh.*

Deciding not to spend an hour explaining a word, Francis took the distraction Ruth offered when she rushed out with a paper bag of biscuits for dog and boy. She fussed over Devlin when his flushed, tear-stained cheeks came into view. She promised to let anyone who asked know the boy had been found safe if Francis didn't catch up to Caddock first.

*Poor lad.*

# Chapter Twenty-Two

CADDOCK

Some moments in life stuck with a person—no matter what followed. Caddock had no doubts this would be one of those times. He clutched his phone, listening to his mother desperately sobbing on the other end.

He hadn't heard her sound like this since his brother had died. His composed, stoic mother never sobbed. For her to lose her composure, something truly awful had to have happened.

"Mother? *Mum.* I can't understand a word you're saying." Caddock pulled the vehicle over to the side of the road. He'd been on his way to visit Rupert when the call had come in. It wouldn't be wise to risk an accident. "What's happened? Where's Dad? Can he tell me?"

"Run… away." She managed to choke out two words.

He sat up sharply, suddenly every nerve in his body on edge. "Is it Devlin? Where is he? Is he hurt? I need you to talk to me."

After excruciatingly long minutes, his mother managed to compose herself. Caddock finally had his answers. She'd been with Devlin driving to Looe when his father had called. Not expecting anything bad, she had put him on speakerphone.

Not a wise decision in the end. His father had gone on and on about the custody fight. He'd had a few choice words to say about his son. It had all been too much for Devlin.

The boy had been inconsolable. He hadn't believed his grandmother when she promised to take him to his beloved Uncle Boo. When the vehicle had stopped at an intersection, the Devil had gotten himself out of his booster seat and been gone before she could catch him.

*Gone.*

His little Devil.

Right.

First, Caddock would find the lad, who was likely terrified and distraught. And then, he'd spoil him rotten, poor boy. He'd follow this up by pummelling his father into the ground when they next met.

Rallying the troops hadn't taken all that much. Rupert and Graham had immediately hopped in a vehicle to head over to help. Joanne had stayed behind to get on the phone with local authorities to put together a search.

A little lad could easily get lost in the nearby farms. Caddock's greatest fear was Devlin's curiosity leading him too close to the sea. He could swim, but no four-year-old would be much of a match for some of the currents in the water.

The skies had been darkening for the last hour. Devlin didn't care for thunder much. He tended to climb into bed with his uncle if a storm happened at night. He must be terrified outside in this.

Caddock would *never* forgive his father for doing this to his own grandson. They'd all been happy, everything had been set. Why did he have to rock the boat now? Over what? His son's personal relationship preferences?

They needed to sit down and have a long talk. Caddock had let this go on for far too long. He was no longer the only person suffering for his father's ignorance.

He'd put up with it for his mother. But Devlin had been hurt as a result. No more. His father would either change his ways or risk being alienated by both his son and grandson.

His mother would likely have a few words for her husband as well. She tended to avoid arguments, believing them to be uncivilized. She'd hated his rugby for the same reason.

But her grandson? She loved Devlin with a fierceness not to be ignored. Caddock scoffed at the idea of an intervention. But maybe it would be the push to force his father to change.

It took several deep breaths before Caddock had a grasp on his anger. The thought of his beloved little Devil outside in the now pouring rain had his blood boiling. He hated it.

"What is he doing here?" Caddock snapped angrily at his father, who stood beside his mother when he pulled up beside them. She'd stayed in the spot where she'd last seen Devlin. "Why is he here?"

"Devlin is my grandson."

"Now you notice?" Caddock all but roared at him.

His father reared back then pinched the bridge of his nose, looking exhausted. "I love my grandson."

"And what the bloody hell have you done lately, but hurt him?" Caddock started towards his father, but his mother wisely caught him by the arm. He gently lifted her hand away though she firmly kept herself between them. She scolded her husband sternly when he opened his mouth to argue. "It doesn't matter. Devlin is the only damn one who matters right now. I'll deal with your shortcomings later."

"Why couldn't you simply be normal?" His father sounded more exhausted and bewildered than outraged. "Why weren't you like Hadrian?"

"And why couldn't you, as my father, accept me for who I am? Aren't parents supposed to love their children unconditionally?" Caddock spat at him, unable to curb the urge to strike out at the person who had hurt his nephew. "I couldn't give a rip if my choices disgust you. But you had no right to drag little Devlin into this. Haddy would be utterly ashamed of you. He wouldn't piss on you if you were on fire for what you've done to his son."

"*Caddock.*"

He refused to let his mother's horrified whisper sway him from his righteous anger. He met his father's pain-filled eyes without flinching. The man deserved so much more than simply harsh words for the last few days. "One day, Devlin will be old enough to understand all of this. He's going to have many questions for his grandfather. I hope you have answers for him. And maybe, just maybe, he'll be more forgiving than I am."

They searched the immediate area for over an hour without success. Caddock's phone had run out of battery in the middle of this. He decided to head to the cottage to grab his charger and was surprised to find Watson parked outside of it.

Ignoring his parents, who had followed, Caddock walked up to the gate, only to freeze in place when he spotted a welcome sight seated on the steps in front of the cottage. He fumbled desperately with the latch, finally leaping over the gate when it wouldn't cooperate with him. He had one thing— one person—on his mind.

"Uncle Boo." Devlin shot out of Francis's arms. He raced down the path and threw himself at his uncle. "Uncle Boo. *Uncle Boo!* Fwannie and Lock founded me. I got lost. I miss you. Don't go away. Pwease don't go away 'gain."

Caddock held the boy, who almost immediately dissolved into broken sobs. Devlin went on and on about never leaving him "like Daddy did." The horrified gasp behind him let him know his parents had heard. It gave him a mildly vindictive thrill.

"Devlin." His grandfather's voice caused the lad to shrink in Caddock's arms. He hid his face against his shirt when they turned around. "Devlin? Lad?"

"Go 'way." Devlin stuck his thumb in his mouth, something Caddock hadn't seen him do in several months as he'd begun to heal from the loss of his beloved father. This turmoil had clearly set him back in the grieving process. "I wanna stay with Uncle Boo."

"I see." His father stepped closer, flinching and paling when Devlin pulled away from the hand that reached out towards him. "I won't take you away from your Uncle Boo."

"You pwomise?" Devlin spoke around his thumb. His eyes were filled with tears still. He sounded so *small*, Caddock wanted to hide him away from the world. "You pwomise, Gwandad?"

He rested a hand gently on the lad's back. "I promise you I won't do it again. And I'm dreadfully sorry for having hurt either of you. I care about you both dearly."

"'Kay." His nephew, who normally showed his emotions overtly and enthusiastically, simply nodded. "Tired."

His parents left after kissing their grandson, deciding the lad needed some alone time with his uncle. He promised to call later. He and his father needed to have a long overdue chat.

Gathering Devlin up closer, Caddock ushered him and Francis into the house. His nephew was understandably clingy, but seemed happy to have Francis and his dog with them. They settled in the living room with mugs of hot chocolate and biscuits.

It was only then Caddock noticed the scratches on Francis's hands. His slender fingers had splotches of dried blood. He immediately retrieved a warm wet cloth and first-aid kit from the bathroom.

Caddock tended first to the scratches on Devlin and then the ones on Francis. He had them tell him all about their adventurous day. He made sure his nephew understood how dangerous running away had been.

A physically and emotionally exhausted Devlin fell into a deep sleep rather quickly after that. Caddock tucked him into his bed then returned to the living room where Francis seemed lost in thought. He took a seat on the couch before dragging Francis into his lap, arms wrapped tightly around him.

"Thank you. I can't thank you enough for bringing him back to me." Caddock buried his nose into Francis's wild brown hair. He chuckled before pulling out a twig. "You're going to need a long bath after this."

"Want to help me wash again?" Francis blushed at his own cheekiness. He shifted around, getting more comfortable in his embrace. "The poor lad was so upset when I found him. Will your father leave it alone after this?"

Caddock let his head fall back against the cushion with a groan. He honestly had no idea if this had knocked sense into his stubborn father. He could only hope Devlin's tear-stained face had some sort of impact. "Maybe. I won't let him go over to their house again unless this is resolved. I won't risk his emotional state for all this adult shit."

"So… bath?" Francis grimaced at the dirt under his nails. "I smell like pasture. It is *not* pleasant."

"We haven't christened my shower yet." Caddock broke into what felt like his first real grin in days. "How silent can you be, cub?"

Silence turned out to be unnecessary. Devlin interrupted them before they could even begin. He stumbled down the hall in his footie pyjamas, dangling his bear behind him. It took a while to settle the lad down.

Three stories, a warm glass of milk, and snuggling down with Sherlock finally did it. With him down finally, hopefully without another nightmare, the two men withdrew to the living room with tea. They held hands, drank their comfort, and enjoyed the now roaring fire.

*This,* Caddock thought, *this is how family and a happy life together could be.*

# Chapter Twenty-Three

CADDOCK

It took days for Devlin to return to his normal self. He refused to go anywhere without his uncle. It hadn't seemed a terrible idea to indulge the lad. What could it hurt?

*Damn Father and his ignorant, outdated shit.*

Insecurity had plagued Devlin's dreams in particular. Every night had been filled with restless sleep and whimpering cries. Caddock would comfort his nephew while mentally visualizing visiting revenge on his father—a healthy pastime in his opinion.

But he knew he would never strike the man, no matter how tempting. Devlin wouldn't thank him for it in any case. The boy still loved his granddad, even if he was a "meanie head from meanie village."

And, after all, Devlin mattered most to everyone involved. Even the hint of legal action had hurt him; physical retribution would only serve to exacerbate the situation. Cool heads were needed to handle this intricate and delicate family issue.

It stopped now. Caddock decided it was time to visit his parents to settle things. His mother had a point when she'd told him sacrificing his urge for payback could only benefit his nephew. Devlin needed his whole family; so somehow, Caddock had to find a way to get through to his father—to make him understand without it devolving into a screaming match or worse.

*Hopefully.*

With Devlin in the garden with his grandmother, it was time to hash things out. Caddock went to his father's office, which brought back so many memories from childhood. He remembered all the times he'd stood in the far left corner with his nose pressed into the dark wood panelling.

Hadrian, of course, often stood in the opposite corner. They'd been close as children. When one was in trouble, the other usually followed along.

The brothers never let anything come between them. It was one of the reasons Caddock felt so strongly about keeping his nephew safe. He was protecting his brother's legacy.

Pictures lined the walls of the small office, which had always felt more of a library than anything else. His father had a deep love of books, something Hadrian and his son shared with the man. It *hadn't* been one of his.

Caddock had never been as close as his brother was to their father. They had similar loves of knowledge and learning.

Haddy was almost the spitting image of the man. He had been the changeling child—never quite fitting in with a family of intellectuals.

And yet, family did matter to him. It did. Nothing mattered more than trying to keep everything together for one special four-year-old. Devlin deserved his complete family.

They owed more to him. The adults had been the ones to bugger it all up. They would have to be the ones to fix the mess.

"Son."

Caddock started in surprise at his father's voice. He gripped the arms of the chair, momentarily brought back to his teen years and the long lectures on his behaviour. Only, he wasn't fearful any longer. He sat up straighter—the picture of a confident man. "It's time for our chat."

They didn't exchange their usual handshake. Caddock crossed his arms and merely stared at the hand held out to him. He wouldn't be drawn into the trap of following simply because family tradition demanded it. Things had to change drastically before he'd show any deference to his father.

His father crossed the room to stand by the tall windows that looked out over the garden. Devlin's happy giggle could be heard from outside. "Such a sweet boy."

"He's all Haddy."

"Yes, indeed."

"You let him down." Caddock left unsaid how much the man had disappointed both of his sons—not only his grandson. "He loves you. Always looks up to you, and you hurt him. He's a forgiving child, doesn't hold a grudge. Haddy could be like that at times. Never stayed angry with someone he loved."

"He had you to do it for him." His father moved over to a nearby cabinet to pour them both a drink. "Hadrian inherited my quiet intellectual mind and your mother's ability to quickly forgive and forget wrongdoings. He was obsessed with all things theoretical. And you, ever the little brute, theory bored you to tears. You could never forgive anyone or forget anything. I often feared the words weren't in your vocabulary at all."

"Thanks."

As character assessments went, it wasn't necessarily wrong, but no one enjoyed hearing their own father point out their flaws. The man always had rose-tinted glasses for Hadrian—his golden child. Caddock could never measure up.

"You get it from your mother's family. It's in the family motto." His father offered him one of the drinks in his hand. "I don't wish for us to be constantly in conflict with one another. Can't you forgive me?"

Caddock had no answer, so taking a sip of Scotch seemed a better idea. They glared at each other—one obstinate prat to another. Forgiveness, for all his father's words, didn't come easily to either of them.

"Well?" his father prompted impatiently. "Can we move on?"

"I'm dating a man." Caddock noted the way his father gulped down his Scotch. He raised an eyebrow at his obvious discomfort. "He's special, my Francis. Devlin loves him. I think… maybe one day, we could be a family together. I have hope."

"*Caddock.*"

"He makes me happy." He refused to shy away from the real issue at hand. It would never be resolved if they didn't face it. "I won't give him up to satisfy your stiff-shirted…."

*Stop. Don't do anything you'll regret. Think calm thoughts. Don't break your glass or your dad's jaw, or his jaw with your glass.*

"I'm sorry."

"And?" Caddock set the tumbler of Scotch down to avoid shattering it against a wall. "What exactly are you sorry about? And how does it fix a bloody thing?"

"Language."

It was so typical of his father. He never wanted to confront issues without deflecting to the superficial. Life felt too short to allow things to be sidetracked by idiotic things like cursing.

"Oh, sod my language. I'm your son. Do you love me or not? Do you love your grandson or not?" Caddock had officially and completely run out of patience with the man. He clenched his fists at his side. "Well? Do you? How deep does your love for your family run?"

Silence reigned in the cramped room for several long minutes. Caddock tried not to make any painful assumptions based on the obvious lack of immediate response. He went through the hurt solely for Devlin's benefit. He'd go through fire for his nephew.

"Is this man the one who found our Devlin?" His father barely restrained his sneer. He absentmindedly poured himself a second drink, turning away from his son's indignant snarl. "Francis, was it? The foppish one?"

He slowed his breathing down and slowly rolled his shoulders to ease the tension. "Why am I here?"

"Be reasonable."

"Fuck reasonable." Caddock was on his feet, towering over his father. He smacked himself in the chest with his fist, over his heart. "I am your son. Does my sexuality really change who I am and how you feel about me? Is it really so important? Who gives a damn who I have in my bed? I'm *your* son. Doesn't that count for anything?"

"I…"

"Mother is in the garden." Caddock stepped away from the man before he said or did something he might regret later on, once his temper had cooled. "I'll say goodbye. Devlin won't want to miss tea with Francis and Sherlock."

"Son." His father caught him by the back of his shirt. He held his son by the arm to keep him from leaving. "I love you."

"Even with my abnormalities?" Caddock refused to be the only one to give an inch. "Can you handle Christmas dinners with my boyfriend? Or will you sneer at him? Poking theoretical holes in our relationship until things are so strained the holiday and every other moment together as a family are miserable and pointless."

"For my son? And my grandson? I will welcome your Francis with open arms, without a shadow of a doubt." His father returned to watching the rest of their family out the window. "We almost lost you once."

"What?" Caddock blinked in confusion at the sudden change of topic. "What are you on about?"

"You were maybe two years old. It happened on Boxing Day. You'd stolen a handful of fruit-flavoured hard sweets, but one of them became stuck in your throat." He closed his eyes, leaning forward until his forehead rested against the windowpane. "Your lips had turned blue by the time I found you. I shook you upside down, swatting your back until the sweet came loose. Those were the longest minutes of my life. I feared I was watching your last breaths. That I had failed as a father."

"Dad." He could see his shoulders trembling slightly. His father never showed emotion—let alone tears. "I forgive you."

"You shouldn't."

"Pardon?"

His father barked out a deep laugh, one so similar to his own. It was the only thing they shared. "My actions of late have been unforgiveable. I will make it up to you and to Devlin. My family is far more important than my discomfort. I am sorry, Caddock. You were right. Hadrian would've flayed me alive for my treatment of you and his son."

*Well, then.*

He had no memory of the event, not surprising given his age. Boxing Day had often been a solemn event for his father. He would lock himself in his office, ignoring everyone. Now he finally understood the reason behind it.

Caddock did return the embrace when his father grabbed him for a second time. He could remember a time when the man had seemed seven feet tall. Nowadays, it was his turn to stand head and shoulders above him.

"Haddy would be proud of you." Caddock waved at Devlin,

who had spotted them through the window. His mother had obviously seen them hugging since she was surreptitiously wiping her eyes. "Devlin will need both of us in his life."

"Of course, he does. You'll never be able to teach him useful things like budgeting or an appreciation for Shakespeare and the arts." He clapped his son on the back. "Enough emotional rubbish for one day. Go see your mother."

Letting his father have time to collect himself, Caddock made his way out into the garden. His mother gave him a tearful "Thank you," and a hug. She went in to start a light lunch while he entertained his nephew.

"Uncle Boo?" Devlin lifted up a small pebble he'd found. "Are you and Gwandad all happy again? Is he done being a meanie?"

"I believe so." Caddock chuckled. He led Devlin over to the pond at the base of the garden to show him how to skip stones. "Your grandfather loves you, Devlin."

"'Kay. Will he give me bickies then?"

*Ahh, the priorities of childhood.*

"I'm sure you can convince him to give you some of his special shortbread biscuits. He's very fond of them." He lifted the boy up into his arms, hefting him on his shoulder. They climbed up the hill to the house where his father stood waiting. "Why don't you go ask?"

"*Gwandad!*" Devlin took off at a run once he'd been set down on the grass. He clutched his grandfather around the knees. "Are you not mad at Uncle Boo? Can we have bickies? Did you say sowwy? Fwannie told me sowwy is what you say when you do something bad."

"Well, your Francis is correct." His grandfather crouched down and rested a hand on his grandson's shoulder. "I am very sorry to have hurt you and your uncle. I know he loves you so much and takes good care of you. And I'm proud of how you stood up for him."

"Does that mean I can have bickies?"

"It means you can have two biscuits." He pulled his grandson into his arms. "You're a wonderful lad. Your father would be proud of you as well."

# Chapter Twenty-Four

FRANCIS

"Light blue, pale blue, or antique blue?" Francis held up three of his many bow ties to his captive audience of one—Sherlock. His dog nosed the pale blue one then licked it. "A brilliant choice. You have good taste."

His giggling gran had delivered a package to him earlier that Caddock had left on their doorstep. He'd carefully unwrapped the brown paper to discover an antique, carved mahogany chest. Inside, he'd found an invitation to dinner, handwritten on thick parchment in fancy calligraphy.

The chest itself Francis recognized as an early nineteenth-century tea caddy. The workmanship of intricately carved inlays on the sides and top were exquisite. He could smell hints of tea on the inside from the years of use.

# After the Scrum

The box now sat on a shelf above his bed. Caddock had gone above and beyond for a simple date invitation. He'd never had a man go so out of his way to impress.

*Charming prat.*

"He did good, Sherlock." Francis stood on his bed to touch a hand to his new antique. He lightly caressed the sleek, aged wood. "Do you think he's going to stay around?"

Sherlock barked twice, tail wagging against the floor.

"Me too." He grimaced when Sherlock rubbed against his trousers—he'd have fur everywhere at this rate. "You are a shaggy menace."

The invite had specifically been for him only. Sherlock would have to be content with Gran for the evening. He doubted the dog would be thrilled with staying home.

His gran had been in to see him several times already during the getting-ready process. "Don't wear the plaid, love. You'll look twice your age in it." Francis didn't necessarily see looking older as a bad thing.

Only *his* gran would be worried about his looking too old. *Honestly.* Francis happened to be in the beginnings of a relationship with a man over ten years his senior. A youthful appearance didn't do *anything* for either of them.

On his fourth attempt to tie his bowtie, Francis threw it onto the dresser in sheer frustration. He hated how Caddock always had an effect on his nerves. Tying knots had never been an issue before, only when his brute was involved.

Caving to the inevitable, Francis found his gran knitting in front of the telly. She gave him a teasing smile before helping with his tie. She smoothed down his wild hair then sent him on his way, promising to keep an eye on Sherlock.

His beloved dog had a tendency to sneak out to track him down if Francis dared go anywhere without him. Not that he went many places without his sheltie. He'd followed him to a neighbouring village once when Francis had dared to go antiquing on his own. Gran would have to watch him like a hawk.

"You look lovely." She watched him brush dog hair from his "not the plaid dear" jacket. "He'll be staring at your bottom all evening in those tight trousers."

"*Gran.*" He blinked at her in horrified bewilderment. She always loved to keep him off balance with her occasionally bawdy sense of humour. "And I am *not* lovely."

"Yes, love, you are." She glanced over her shoulder then returned to her partially completed scarf—Ravenclaw colours for Devlin's favourite Hogwarts' house. "You tell him to come over with his little lad for tea tomorrow. I'll have this finished by then."

"Yes, Gran."

"I won't be waiting up, so if you come back, be sure to lock the gate behind you." She looked far too knowing for his liking, but experience told him to leave her to her laughter. "Enjoy yourself."

"Yes, Gran."

"Use protection."

"Yes… *Gran!*" His face flushed several shades of pink when her words registered. He gave her a quick hug before dashing out the door before she could say anything else. "Horrifying woman."

# After the Scrum

He was thankful for the jacket when the crisp sea breeze hit him. Caddock stood by his vehicle, leaning against it with a playful smile on his face. He casually perused Francis from head to toe without bothering to hide his blatant leer.

"Miss me?"

"I've seen you almost every day this week." Francis stepped forward into the broad arms that were held out to him. "Gran wants you to come for tea tomorrow with Devlin."

"Because the Devil needs more spoiling."

"She thinks so and she is *never* wrong." Francis found himself ushered into the vehicle after a trouser-tightening kiss. "Where are we going?"

"You'll see." Caddock appeared to think on something quite seriously before continuing. "I might blindfold you to heighten the surprise."

"I am *not* a kinky man."

"No?" Caddock's hand rested heavily on Francis's thigh. "How do you know until we've tried it? There are so many flavours to experiment with. It would be a shame to wash your hands of it all before even dipping your toes in the water."

Deciding no comment would be better than stumbling over his own words, Francis turned stubbornly towards watching where they were headed. He'd expected to eat at one of the fancier restaurants in town, or perhaps at the cottage. Devlin was staying with Joanne and Rupert—he hadn't wanted to go to his grandparents.

It would take time to heal the rift with their grandson. Francis thought the apologies had gone a long way towards it, but Devlin appeared reticent to stay on his own with them, likely residual fear of being taken from his uncle. Children were remarkably resilient; he would likely be back to normal in no time.

It would be the adults who had the worst of it. Francis knew underneath it all, Caddock had yet to fully forgive his father. And as change rarely came easily, the man likely would struggle to truly let go of his previous discomfort so easily. Work would be required to keep the family together.

A sudden U-turn had them heading towards the sea, of all places. The weather wasn't the warmest on record. It was distinctly chilly, in fact. The particular road they were on led to a private little cove, beautiful in the day. He'd never been there during twilight hours.

They made a strange procession down towards the sea once they arrived. Caddock insisted on covering Francis's eyes with his hands. They shuffled in an awkward manner along the twisted, pebble-covered path.

After five minutes of stumbling, cursing, laughing, and then stumbling again, the two men made it down to the seashore relatively safely. Francis had a bruise on his hip from bumping into a large jagged rock. They continued chuckling at each other until Caddock finally lifted his hands away.

Francis found himself standing on the sands of Lantic Bay near a massive bonfire. Off to one side of it were two chairs, blankets, and a small hamper.

"It's only sandwiches and a thermos of tea." Caddock gestured towards the darkening sky. "You said you wanted to watch the meteor shower tonight. It's a clear night. We might freeze our bollocks off, but there you are."

164

"Oh." Francis had actually forgotten about the cosmic event. "Brilliant. How on earth did you remember something I briefly mentioned the day we met?"

"You were memorable. I'm fairly certain I can remember every damn bit of our conversation—pathetic really." He shrugged with a self-deprecating smile.

"Did you suddenly uncover a romantic bone underneath all the muscle?" Francis teased then tried to dodge Caddock's arm, which swung out towards him. He jumped when a large hand smacked him on his arse. His body responded with avid interest to the warm tingling left behind. He searched for something to distract from it. "What? Where are my roses? Actually, no poncey flowers for me, thanks. I'd take chocolate though. Where's my chocolate?"

"*Cub.*"

Francis pointedly ignored the way he reacted to the deep timbre in one single, innocent word. His partner didn't need any more of an ego boost. "Well? Is there a plan—aside from freezing our bollocks off?"

Caddock's eyes narrowed at yet another sudden shift in topic. His voice remained low and gravelly. "I *always* have a plan. Sandwiches and tea first, I think. You'll need your strength."

"I will?"

A gentle shove had him collapsing back into one of the chairs. Caddock draped a thick blanket over his lap. Seconds later, he held a steaming mug of tea along with his favourite sandwich—cheese and tomato with chive-flavoured butter.

Dragging the second seat closer, Caddock sat down with

his long legs stretched out in the sand. They ate and sipped tea in relative silence, enjoying the sound of the water lapping at the shore, the whistling wind and crackling fire. It was a perfect date, even with the nippy weather.

As the sun finally disappeared, Francis's anticipation steadily grew. They had at least an hour before the spectacular dramatics in the sky would start. He had no doubts his lover had a few ideas on how to pass the time. Caddock could be incredibly inventive.

*Incredibly. Inventive.*

When the cups and plates had been returned to the hamper, Caddock knelt in front of him. His strong hands gripped Francis by the knees. His legs were slowly parted while thumbs teasingly caressed him through his trousers.

"Someone could see. The cove is a popular destination, after all…. *Caddock.* Are you even listening to me?" Francis shivered when those fingers began to trail along the inseam of his trousers. He glared at the kneeling man. "This isn't exactly priv—"

A sharp flick against his inner thigh silenced him. Francis bit his bottom lip when the same hand brushed against his groin for the first time. He gave in to the touches, drifting off on a sea of heightened enjoyment.

Why fight it?

Saints above though, Francis hoped no one would decide to take a midnight stroll. He didn't want to be any more infamous than the tabloid had made him. *Oh, God. How does he do that with one finger?*

*Or that?*

# After the Scrum

"*Caddock.*" Francis couldn't help lifting his hips up when Caddock abruptly withdrew his hand—searching for the touches to continue. "If you stop now, I swear on Watson, I'll allow Sherlock to take a piss in Dr Evil."

"Naughty cub." He flicked Francis's inner thigh again. He seemed to find the sharp intakes of breath highly amusing. His hands rose higher and higher, closer to the hardening, overly interested part of Francis's anatomy. "And you said you weren't kinky."

Any attempt at response faded in a fog of pleasure. Caddock distracted him with a hard kiss and before Francis realized it, his trousers and pants were shoved down to his ankles. The blast of cold shocked him. He shivered at the chill before Caddock's warm breath wafted across him—causing shivers for a completely different reason.

The breath inched closer until the first lick teased him lightly. Tentative swipes of the tongue eventually became longer and more encompassing. Francis lost his ability to think rationally when he was swallowed whole.

Caddock hummed while he moved up and down, sending intense vibrations through Francis. He would've bucked wildly, but firm arms pressed down on the top of his thighs. He lost himself to desire while his hands gripped the blanket at his side.

The moment of blinding pleasure hit him fast and hard. By the time Francis could form a coherent thought, a thick, slick finger had inched its way into him. It twisted around inside.

The wind still whistled around them while the stars shone overhead. It was all too surreal. He couldn't believe he was half-starkers under a moonlit sky.

One finger became two almost too soon. It burned. Oh, how it burned sweetly. Francis shifted down in his seat, hoping to entice Caddock to do more.

"Please...." He wanted the fingers to be replaced by something better and larger. "Caddock. You teasing prat. Give me more. Are you trying to drive me to the edge of insanity?"

"Better be quiet, cub." Caddock scissored his fingers before thrusting them deeper. "We wouldn't want an audience. Or would you? What hidden desires can I drag out of you? How many wonderfully twisted fantasies are hidden behind those blue eyes?"

Francis valiantly tried to maintain some sort of composure, only to have a casual movement from Caddock dash away all his attempts. "Anything—just give me something."

And there went all those plans of playing hard to get. The talented mouth had been busy bringing Francis back to life. His fingers were incessant in their torment. How could they feel so brilliant, yet pale in comparison to the man himself, to what he truly longed for?

The fingers finally eased out of him. They spread and turned repeatedly all the way. He disliked the sudden emptiness. A soft flick to his already most sensitive spot sent shockwaves up his spine.

*Bloody hell.*

It shouldn't have felt as good as it did. And the second tap definitely shouldn't have turned him to a pile of mush. Francis wondered absently if he would die of too much pleasure on the beach with his trousers down.

It might make for an interesting obituary.

His mind blanked once again when something rather larger than a finger bumped against his entrance. Caddock put a condom on then slid all the way to his hilt in one smooth press. He bent over Francis until their lips hovered over one another.

"God. Fucking brilliant." Caddock hissed while shaking with the effort to hold himself still above the Francis. His tongue swiped at Francis's lips, darting in when they parted for him. "Did I say how fucking brilliant you feel?"

"Pun intended?"

"You cheeky cub." Caddock thrust hard then drew almost all the way out. "Fucking chair."

With a suspiciously practiced air, Caddock flourished out the blanket to drape over the sand before the fire. He carried Francis over to it, situating him on his back. Strong hands rested on either side of his body, and he took his time driving in once more.

Caddock brought a hand up to drag across the lithe chest underneath him. He paid great attention to any spot that made Francis move. "Just like that, cub. Move with me."

Not even the bitterly cold air could deter Francis's enjoyment at all. He found a perfect rhythm with Caddock above him. Their lips met, silencing both of their moans. It wouldn't be long—couldn't be.

"God, yes."

"Harder."

And then finally, the completion they'd both been chasing. They collapsed on their banks on the blanket, gasping for air.

He found himself staring up at the brightly lit sky. The meteor shower had started.

"See? I took you to outer space." Caddock grunted when Francis dug his elbow into his side. "Was that really necessary?"

# Chapter Twenty-Five

FRANCIS

It had been a perfect night. They'd stayed up into the wee hours of the morning to watch the sun rise. They'd been damn near frozen as well—blankets and body heat only did so much.

The fire had dwindled almost to nothing by the time they started the short hike back up to the Range Rover. Francis found the trek much easier without hands covering his eyes. Caddock still managed to trip him up several times. He seemed far too amused by trying to flick his lover's arse.

*Prat.*

Since Caddock was in a rush to check in on Devlin, Francis asked him to drop him off. He didn't want to delay returning home much longer. Staying out all night had been enough; any further waiting would only incite his gran further. She was going to be insufferable as it was.

Francis stopped at his cottage *only* to pick up Sherlock. Gran's knowing looks were too much to handle at eight in the morning. He hadn't had tea yet. No amount of teasing could be dealt with without at least one cup.

*"You do look rather flushed, love. Long night out at the cove?"*

With Caddock at his pub with Rupert, Joanne, and Graham, Francis had opted to go to his office. He had other clients, after all. Those four along with Devlin could easily finish up the last details before the bar opening at the end of the week.

Tea and a scone were happily provided by Ruth. She had a teasing glint in her eyes. Gossip had apparently already reached her ears. Thank God no one knew *precisely* what had happened on the beach. He'd be blushing until eternity.

Slipping Sherlock a sliver of the scone, Francis grabbed the post on the floor. He flipped through it briefly, eventually stowing it away in his bag. It held nothing of vital importance that required his immediate attention.

The morning had been so pleasant, yet Francis couldn't shake the uneasy feeling in the pit of his stomach. For once, Sherlock trailed behind him. He trudged up the stairs to his office. Maybe the scone had given him indigestion.

And then it happened.

He'd barely crossed the threshold when the door slammed shut behind him. Sherlock whined then pawed at the door, obviously becoming increasingly frantic. The dog's barking grew louder, only to stop altogether seconds later. Francis spun around, to find himself shoved up against a wall by an obviously drunk Patty.

"I saw you." He swayed on his feet, but his strength was surprisingly sufficient to hold his captive in place. "Saw you on the beach with that new bloke."

*Shit.*

*I'm going to kill Caddock.*

*If I survive.*

"You're filthy." Patty licked a disgusting swath along his neck. "I like filthy."

"Get off me." Francis struggled against him, but then the man's putrid breath hit him. It choked him—his throat closing tightly at the stark reminder of his worst night years ago. The terrifying walls of anxiety closed on him. He practically wilted at the onslaught of memories. "No. *No.*"

It was his living nightmare. The one thing Francis prayed never to have happen to him *ever* again. The reason he had never visited London again, unless forced by circumstances. Why now? Why him?

A forceful shake caused him to whack his head against the wooden panelling that made up the walls of his office. Francis slid to the floor with a pained groan. He skittered away from the stumbling man, trying to find refuge.

He barely made it halfway to his desk when a gnarled hand grabbed his ankle. Patty dragged him over, and Francis shrank away from the drunk. This would not end well.

The walls closed in as always while his breath came in short gasps. His panic attack refused to wait for a more convenient time. Francis shivered while trying to find some semblance of control.

"You're a pretty bloke." Patty stood over him, a disgusting

leer on his face. "Not handsome. You sure you're a bloke?"

He cringed at the touch on his ankles, desperately trying to yank himself out of the grasp. He would *not* be weak this time. Not again. *Never* again.

"You *will* release me." Francis strived to find strength in his faltering voice. "I said… *release* me."

"Or what?" Patty didn't appear at all concerned by the threats. "Pretty lads like you don't stand a chance with a real man. What're you gonna do to me?"

Francis had no answer for his slurred question. Patty went for him again. He struggled to get free of the man. He would *not* tremble in fear, waiting for rescue.

Kicking his way free, Francis struggled to his feet. The early whack to his head and the panic attack made him almost as unsteady as the drunk. He struggled across the small office, trying to get free.

He made it to the door, only to be yanked back. Patty knocked him to the floor and Francis's head caught the edge of his heavy antique desk. The world went dark.

# Chapter Twenty-Six

CADDOCK

Busy—the one word that described Caddock's morning perfectly. He thought perhaps frantically busy might be more accurate. The bar opening in a couple days had him running ragged.

The staff had been hired, and thankfully, were all experienced enough not to need training. They might end up being the ones training him. He'd brought in two bartenders, a chef, and a manager to help him keep the place from descending into chaos.

Haddy's was a small enough pub not to need a massive number of employees. The chef wanted to hire at least one more person in the kitchen. Caddock had ended up taking in a local lad who needed part-time work while attending university.

Rupert, Graham, and Joanne had all come to help him with the last-minute touches in the pub. Joanne had *mostly* been directing the three men and helping to corral Devlin. Granted, the lad got into less trouble than the overgrown boys did. Caddock knew from experience she could deal with them as easily as the four-year-old.

"Watch, Uncle Boo. *Watch!*" Devlin gave a happy shriek, making all the adults wince at the piercing sound. "Uncle Boo!"

Caddock paused while balancing two boxes of pint glasses to dutifully watch Devlin balance on Graham's shoulders. "I see. Oi, blond one, you break him, you bought him."

"How much for him?" Graham held the boy up on his shoulders while rooting around his pocket. "I've got a few quid somewhere in here. How about it?"

"Bad Gwaham." Devlin boxed the man over his ears then quickly apologized when his uncle frowned at him. He giggled when Rupert told him not to worry about it; his brother's head was too hard to damage easily. "Lock, Lock, Lock."

Setting down the boxes, Caddock watched in bewilderment when Sherlock dashed up to him. The dog snatched the edge of his trousers in his teeth and attempted to drag him towards the open door. The adults all glanced towards it, expecting Francis to appear. He would never let the sheltie wander too far away on his own.

They waited.

And *waited.*

"It's like an episode of Lassie," Rupert muttered. Sherlock grew more frantic, almost nipping Caddock's leg.

176

"Which one?" Graham asked offhandedly.

"Pick one. They all started like this."

"Is now really the time?" Joanne swatted her husband on the arm. She snatched Devlin from her brother-in-law. Her sharp words caught their attention, which had likely been her intention. "It might be wise if you three follow him. Sherlock's a smart dog. He wouldn't leave Francis unless something was truly wrong. He's been trained to stick with his owner. Well? Get on with it then."

"Does she order you about in bed too?" Caddock dodged the punch Rupert threw at him. He turned to Sherlock and started for the door. "C'mon, you mangy creature, lead the way. But if Francis is fine and dandy, you're in the doghouse."

The three men had to jog to keep Sherlock in sight. He would race forward then dart back to ensure they didn't lose track of him. It didn't take long to reach Francis's office.

They found Ruth hovering by the outer door to the building, worry evident on her face. Her hands gripped her apron tightly. The icy fingers of dread spread in Caddock's gut. His heart started to race and he went from jogging to full on sprinting.

"We heard—I'm not sure—it sounded like boxes falling or a fight. My Stevie's trying to get into the office." Ruth stepped out of their way then crouched down to wrap her arms around Sherlock's neck. "I'll keep the little love out from under your feet. Go on up. Hurry now."

Taking the stairs two at a time, Caddock waved Stevie out of his way from where the man had been trying to pick the lock. He used his shoulder as a battering ram to crash through the door. The three behind him followed quickly into the room.

They stopped, momentarily stunned by the sight of a man—the drunk Caddock had seen weeks earlier outside his pub—standing over an unconscious Francis. *Patty? Isn't that his name?* He appeared almost confused by the limp body at his feet.

Caddock launched himself at the bastard when he spotted drying blood on his lover's head. He knocked Patty to the floor. Rupert and Stevie moved quickly to pull him away while Graham easily caught the drunk to restrain him.

"No killing the arsehole, Brute. Let the coppers deal with him." Rupert motioned to Stevie, whose angry flashing eyes belied his normal gentle giant face. "Give the police a call? We're going to need an ambulance. Caddock—see if you can get Francis to wake up, but don't let him move."

With several shaky breaths, Caddock managed to pull back the blinding haze of rage. A skittering of claws on the wooden floor told him Sherlock had wriggled away from Ruth. The dog plastered himself on his owner, quietly whinging and licking his face.

"Sherlock."

The pained whisper was music to Caddock's ears. He dropped to his knees beside Francis. A gentle nudge had Sherlock sitting to the right instead of directly on his owner. They didn't know how hurt he was, after all.

Caddock brought up his hand to smooth the ruffled chaos of Francis's hair. His fingers trembled while he gently searched for any injuries. He found two impressive goose eggs on the man's head—not a good sign.

"Are you hurt anywhere other than your head?" Caddock kept his voice soft, not wanting to spook Francis into a panic attack. He could hear the sirens growing closer. They'd at least have professional medical help soon. "Your Sherlock pulled a Lassie."

"Did he? I owe him a biscuit." Francis seemed to slowly be returning to himself. He turned his head away, blushing as if ashamed. Sherlock gave him a comforting lick. "Maybe Ruth will make a large peanut butter one for you."

"The paramedics are here," Rupert called over to them before Francis could continue praising his dog. "Don't terrify the coppers, Brute. You hear me? Be nice, they're here to help."

"I fought back this time."

For a second, Caddock simply stared at a dazed Francis on the floor in confusion. *What?* It dawned on him finally, after remembering Francis's comments about the attack in London. He'd clearly wanted to feel in control—to save himself this time around.

Reminding himself murder was still considered illegal helped his returning rage at the thought of how much this might set the still healing man back. Caddock smiled at Francis. He told him how proud he should be of himself.

He left out there had been no reason for shame on his part for either attack. The only ones who deserved recriminations were the bastards who'd attacked Francis. He would remind him of it after the head injury had been examined.

"It didn't change anything." Francis winced when the paramedic began carefully inspecting him for injuries. "I don't need a hospital."

"*Cub.*" Caddock glared sternly at him. No way in hell would Francis *not* be getting a full check-up by a doctor. "Let the nice paramedics make sure you didn't turn your brain into runny eggs."

"You think you're funny." Francis didn't have the strength to fully express his annoyance.

The paramedics left no room for further comment. They eased Francis onto a stretcher. Caddock followed with Sherlock close behind him.

He nodded absently to the police, who had already escorted Patty into the back of one of their vehicles. One of the detectives took his number and promised to follow up with him later. They seemed to understand his need to follow the ambulance.

"Graham," Caddock yelled out of his vehicle to get the blond's attention. "Have Ruth call Francis's gran. She should hear about this before the damn gossips spread it around."

The man mock saluted before jogging towards the nearby bakery. Caddock gently ruffled Sherlock's fur to soothe the anxious dog. He told himself Francis would be fine—had to be.

*Had to be.*

Unwanted memories of a teammate who died after a head injury came to mind. Caddock had to force himself to ease off the accelerator. A car accident wouldn't be a help to anyone.

Sherlock curled up on the front seat. He appeared as worried as Caddock. No one would rest easy until they knew Francis was fine, relatively speaking.

# After the Scrum

They would all want Francis home—safely. Caddock could spoil him to his heart's content then. Show the man how attached to each other they'd become.

Given how much the entire village loved Francis, there was no doubt he'd be overwhelmed with attention once word got out. The police would need to keep Patty under lock and key for his own safety. No one would take the attack on the eccentric decorator kindly.

"Sherlock? Think you can behave at the A & E? We wouldn't want to get kicked out." Caddock laughed when the dog wagged his tail twice. "Is it twice for yes? And I'm talking to a bloody dog. I have lost my mind. It's official. You've made me go nutters."

Sherlock growled.

"My apologies."

Sherlock wagged his tail again. The dog had an eerie ability to understand at times, probably because Francis talked to him constantly. They were the best of friends.

He wondered if Francis looked on his dog as the one being in his life who never judged him. Grandmothers, like parents, didn't often count into those kinds of considerations. He hoped to prove himself to be another person to rely upon.

By the time Caddock arrived at the emergency room, Francis had been moved to a private room. The doctors were with him, so he sat with Sherlock impatiently in the waiting room, joined eventually by Rupert and Francis's grandmother.

The normally cheerful woman appeared pale and drawn. She sank silently into a chair. Caddock thought her knees might've given out on her. Sherlock immediately moved over to sit by her, resting his head on her leg to offer and receive comfort.

Caddock strode down the hall to find a drink machine. He grabbed a cup of tea to bring back to her. "Francis will be fine. He's a strong man. Stronger than he thinks."

"Oh, I know, dear. I do worry though. You'll watch over him, won't you?" She turned shrewd eyes towards him. Her aged hands gripped the paper cup. "You will, or I'll take a cricket bat to your head. He's my boy. And I can see you care. So you keep caring, understood?"

"Yes, ma'am." Caddock kicked a snickering Rupert in the shin. "I can still—"

"Are you the family of Francis?"

Caddock spun around to find a doctor holding a chart, staring at the three expectantly. The woman frowned at Sherlock when she spotted him. "He's a therapeutic canine—Francis's actually."

"Ahh." She didn't seem overly pleased by the canine in her hospital, but appeared to see the wisdom in letting the matter rest. "Francis is going to be fine. He has a concussion, but from the scans I've done, I don't believe it to be life-threatening. He's going to be disoriented for a while. Given the nature of his trauma, I would advise keeping a close eye on him for a few days. I've prescribed something for the headache, which is likely to linger."

"Can we take him home then?" Rupert asked hopefully.

"We're discharging him now." She nodded.

Gran reached out to touch Caddock's arm lightly. Her

hand shook and Caddock covered it with his own, giving her a comforting squeeze. "Go get our lad."

# Chapter Twenty-Seven

CADDOCK

Francis had surprised his family and friends with his rather speedy recovery. Caddock worried it had been a tad *too* quick. He hadn't been certain it was his place to say anything, but it seemed several hours spent with his therapist had done wonders for his state of mind.

*They hoped.*

The tender care of one persistent four-year-old might have also helped. Devlin hadn't been told any specifics, yet the clever lad instinctively knew something bad happened to his "Fwannie." Shared biscuits, cuddles, and stories were apparently his idea of the perfect cure-all.

Neither Caddock nor Francis had the heart to dissuade the boy. As a result, it had pulled the slightly down man out of his dismal mood. Devlin had a way about him, something he had most certainly inherited from his father.

Haddy would've made a brilliant doctor. He soothed hearts often without even meaning to do so. Instinct had more often than not been his guiding force, something his son did as well. Caddock would have to watch over him closely to keep life from kicking him in the teeth too viciously.

A week had passed since the incident with the drunk. The pub opening had been delayed because of permit issues and they hoped to have it resolved by the following week. While Caddock was aggravated by the delay, it allowed him to spend more time with Francis.

Despite his insistence on being fine, Francis hadn't ventured far from home much. They decided to force the issue, using Devlin to convince him to take Sherlock for a walk with them. Maybe his nephew would end up as a barrister—the boy could argue the Queen out of her crown.

They all managed to agree fresh air would do wonders for any and all ailments. A stroll through Looe would also allow the villagers to see Francis with their own eyes. Everyone had been so concerned for him.

News of the attack had spread like wildfire. The police had actually put Patty in a cell on his own, worried he might be attacked. Francis was loved by all. They hadn't taken his assault well.

"I'm too tired for a walk." Francis was a terrible liar—a blatant one as well. He couldn't meet Caddock's eyes. "I'm simply exhausted—couldn't sleep a wink."

"Good. The walk will tire you out and let you rest better."

Caddock put an end to the argument by simply lifting the man up and carrying him out the door. Devlin raced behind them, giggling at Francis who kept swatting Caddock on the back. "Sherlock needs a walk and so do you. Be a good cub and stop protesting."

"You take him." Francis's protests fell on uninterested ears. He found himself bustled out the door with relative ease. "You're a demanding brute. Thank God you're attractive; otherwise, no one would want to put up with you."

"Want a coffee?"

"Now you're appealing to my baser needs." Francis perked up a bit at the idea.

According to Ruth, who handed Francis coffee and several freshly made custard tarts, her pastries could do miracles. Devlin, with his own bag of peanut butter biscuits to share with Sherlock, wanted to know what miracle meant. The lad asked everyone they met on the street about it. By the time they'd started to turn back for home, everyone including the local priest had offered an opinion.

Devlin found it all incredibly confusing. It made Francis smile. Caddock would've dealt with worse than endless questions for that alone.

They made a slow procession down the cobblestone alley that led towards the sea. Devlin danced along beside Sherlock. The two took turns taking bites of the biscuits. They'd be buzzed on sugar for hours.

*Wonderful.*

"Are you going to share?" Caddock teased. Francis hugged the paper bag containing the custard tarts to his chest. He nodded towards the other one that held the biscuits. "You can have some of those."

"Caring is sharing."

"Says the prat without custard tarts." Francis laughed—his first unbridled one in days. He reached out to take Caddock by the hand. "I'm going to be fine. He left no lingering damage. My panic attacks are no better and no worse. You can stop waiting for me to shatter."

"If you do splinter into a million pieces, I'm gifted with superglue." Caddock winked at him, keeping an eye on Devlin and Sherlock. The two stayed close to them, but he wouldn't put it past them to be getting themselves into trouble. "And for the record, I know you aren't going to shatter."

"Uncle Boo?" Devlin trudged over with the sheltie at his heels. He then tugged on Caddock's sleeve and lifted his hands up. "I'm sweepy."

*Ahh. Nap time.* He'd wondered how long it would take for the boy to get tired. He'd been up rather early. A walk through the village, no matter how small, had clearly taken all his energy reserves.

Lifting his nephew up into his arms, they changed direction to head to the cottage. Caddock found himself imagining they were a family—two fathers, a son, and his dog. The strength of his longing for it hit like a tackle on the rugby pitch.

*Too soon.*

*Damn it all.*

"Caddock?"

He shook his head to clear the images in his mind. "Sorry. Just thinking."

**187**

DAHLIA DONOVAN

"Did it hurt? Wait, I think I can smell smoke coming from your ears." Francis reached up to fan away the smoke. "You might want to grease your wheels."

"Funny. Did you become a comedian overnight?" Caddock kicked his leg up to catch his lover in the arse with his foot. Devlin giggled drowsily with his head resting on his uncle's shoulder. He kept one arm firmly around his nephew while winding his other one around Francis. "I never imagined what moving to Cornwall would bring me. I'm so glad I let Rupert convince me it was a good idea."

"Are you turning into a weepy brute?" Francis leaned into him with a tired sigh. Devlin was apparently not the only one in need of a rest. "I'm incredibly pleased you came as well."

"Are you?" Caddock wiggled his eyebrows with an exaggeratedly lecherous grin.

"Oh, shut it." Francis ruffled Devlin's hair. "The tiny human has big ears. You want to explain the birds and the bees to him this early on?"

"Fair point."

If one looked at the dictionary under idyllic, Caddock felt fairly certain it would show a photo of the four of them. Walking through picturesque Looe, villagers kept popping out to say hello. It was something out of one of those soppy movies his mother loved so much.

*Oh, for.... Get a grip.*

By the time they arrived at the cottage, Devlin had started to snore softly in his ear. His first order of business was to get the lad tucked into bed. Sherlock hopped up to snooze at his feet. The dog had definitely grown attached to his nephew. He

188

seemed as protective over him as he was with his owner.

He quietly walked out of the room, leaving the two to nap together. Life had certainly thrown him for several loops lately. He wondered if Haddy had used his time in the afterlife to screw around with his brother's plans. It was something he would do.

The changes in his life had all—for the most part—been good ones. Caddock wouldn't change a minute of his move to Looe. Even the bad moments that had led him to this.

Sounds coming from the kitchen drew him over. Francis stood by the counter, making tea for both of them. He held out one of the mugs with a tentative smile.

"Hope you don't mind."

Caddock didn't want to terrify Francis by telling him how much he *didn't* mind him making himself at home in his cottage. "No tart?"

"If I must." Francis sighed dramatically. He reluctantly held out a plate with one of the custards. His eyes were alight with suppressed laughter. "Nothing says romance like a shared tart."

"You naughty thing." Caddock swallowed down his urge to roar with laughter. It wouldn't do to wake up Devlin so soon after being put down for some rest. He snatched one of the pastries before Francis could change his mind. "Can you stay for supper?"

"And breakfast?"

"Definitely for breakfast."

Not wanting to press Francis for anything, Caddock decided a cuddle by the fire would be their best plan. Francis grabbed one of the novels from a nearby bookcase before joining him on the sofa. He turned to the first page then held it up.

"You want me to read?"

"You've got the perfect voice for narration—all deep and raw. Read me a story?" Francis settled himself on the couch. He leaned against Caddock, who had an arm around him. "It's such a lovely cottage, all warm. Might be a lark to read together."

Those vulnerable, pleading blue eyes could've probably convinced him to try to fly to the moon. Caddock took a sip of tea, cleared his throat, and then began with the first sentence. By the fourth page, the book started to waver in Francis's hands. The warmth had made them both drowsy.

The novel slipped out of slack fingers. Francis sank further into his embrace. Maybe the adults needed a nap as well.

They stretched out on the sofa. It was a little cramped, but they managed to avoid falling off the edge. Caddock looped his arms around the more slender Francis. His grip shifted them closer until they rested tightly against each other.

Quiet giggles woke Caddock. The soft sound was followed by light pats on his head. He opened his eyes to find Devlin and Sherlock watching them intently.

"Is nap time over then?"

"Uncle Boo?" Devlin scrambled up onto the sofa. His little feet dug into Francis first, and then painfully into his uncle until he managed to snuggle into the space between them. "Is Fwannie gonna stay for beans on toast?"

"He might."

# After the Scrum

Devlin poked Francis on the cheek to get his attention. "Do you want beans on toast?"

"Sounds delightful."

"What's that?" Devlin tilted his head in confusion.

"Yummy." Francis tickled the boy then let out a surprised squeak when he slipped off the edge of the couch to land on the floor. "That was *not* delightful."

Sherlock immediately pounced on him, licking his face and wagging his tail happily. The two rolled on the rug for a few minutes before Francis eventually got to his feet. He told his dog to settle and the sheltie immediately curled up on the nearby armchair.

"Now why can't you be so easy to manage?" Caddock tickled his nephew, who wiggled and giggled wildly. "All right, Devlin, time for beans on toast."

His nephew immediately dove off the couch. He skipped towards the kitchen, popping back to yell for the two adults to follow him. Sherlock seemed content to watch them from his comfortable seat.

Yet another scene straight from some family romance. Caddock found himself enjoying dithering in the kitchen with his nephew and his boyfriend. *Boyfriend? Significant other? Partner?* He scratched his head while carefully watching the melting cheddar on the slices of toast under the grill. He'd yet to find the right description for their relationship.

Caddock had never been fond of *boyfriend*. It felt like something a fourteen-year-old would use. He definitely didn't *look* like a boy anything. Lover felt a little more grown-up. Partner sounded like something his father would say.

*Definitely. Not.*

Shaking his head, Caddock told himself not to overthink any of it. They had only begun the journey together. It wouldn't do to get so wrapped up in defining it so early on. Flexibility had always been important to him, on the rugby pitch and in life.

He caught Francis watching him out of the corner of his eye while also keeping Devlin away from the food cooking on the stove. They truly did work well together. Yet another checked box on finding the perfect person to share his life with.

*You overly romantic sop. Focus on the toast before you burn it. Idiot.*

# Chapter Twenty-Eight

FRANCIS

As the days went by, Francis found his hands shook less. The nightmares faded, not entirely, but enough not to torment him endlessly. He went from speaking to his therapist every day to only twice that week—a vast improvement to his mind.

He'd spent several nights at Caddock's cottage, much to his gran's delight and amusement. He had, in all honesty, expected the man to suffocate him with overprotectiveness. Instead, his desire for space to breathe had been expected.

The simple act of attempting to fight back during his attack had done wonders for his psyche. A ridiculous concept, since Francis logically knew it didn't make him any less traumatized. And yet it helped him immensely.

His therapist had warned him about the dangers of putting

so much stock in having fought back. She worried it would erode his healing progress. After all, freezing during the assault in London didn't make him weak. Francis couldn't quite squash the feeling, no matter how hard he tried.

If Francis were honest with himself, he'd fallen into feeling like a victim after London. He'd given away power over his thoughts. It had been a group attack, his chances of fighting them off had been slim to none, but his recovery process might've been quicker had he made the mental shift from victim to survivor.

At least, his therapist kept telling him it made a difference. Francis *had* thought himself to be weak. Now, he knew better. Patty had been one drunk, and though he'd fought, it hadn't made much of a difference. Perhaps healing could happen, with the knowledge being unable to escape didn't make him less of a person.

"Coffee, love?" His gran broke him out of his thoughts and waved a mug under his nose. "Did you get all your duckies in a row for the pub opening tomorrow?"

"My duckies? Caddock's the one who's opening a pub. I did my work ages ago." Francis didn't find it necessary to mention the hours he'd spent at Haddy's in the last four days. "I do have other clients, Gran."

"Clients? Yes. Other devastatingly handsome rugby players? No." She took a sip of her tea then offered a chunk of scone to Sherlock. Her smile had him covering his face with his hands to hide the sudden blush. "Coy doesn't suit you, love."

"Saints preserve me." Francis pondered briefly the moral

issues with closing the door in her face. "Don't you have a scarf to knit? Or potatoes to peel? Or gossip to share?"

"No need to get narky." She took another casual drink. "You know, your mother used to get so flustered when I asked about her dates with your father. I can see her in you when you blush. It's no wonder the man's fallen so hard for you."

"*Gran.*"

To his eternal gratitude, she took the hint and left him to his coffee in peace. Francis had a few hours before Caddock and Devlin were expecting him. They would be passing out invitations to the local business owners close to the pub for the opening. He didn't completely see the point, since everyone and their mother knew about it.

Given how poplar Caddock had become, the entire legal-aged adult population of Looe would be stopping by the pub the following night for a pint. The way he'd cared for Francis had endeared him to all and sundry. They all hoped Haddy's became a success as a result.

On a selfishly personal level, Francis wanted the pub to work. It would ensure Caddock stayed in the village. He didn't yet feel secure enough in their connection to think the man would remain solely for him.

They had connected so quickly with that strange, almost instantaneous chemistry. Francis worried it would fade into nothing as infatuations often did. But then, Caddock would glance his way at times with such intensity. Maybe there was more depth than he dared hope.

Before Francis could further devolve into obsessing about their relationship, Sherlock roused himself and began his

I-demand-a-walk dance. Francis caved to the inevitable and quaffed down his coffee quickly. His persistent companion happily trotted behind him, herding him out of the bedroom.

Francis tried to duck out without drawing attention to himself. A quiet, "Say hello to your lad," followed him out the door. He pinched the bridge of his nose with a sigh, glaring half-heartedly down at Sherlock.

"This is all your fault."

Sherlock barked at him.

"Glad we settled that." Francis ignored the look from the milkman next door. He'd been living in Looe for most of his life; they should be used to him talking to animals. He waved at the man with a smile. "It's only worrisome if Sherlock starts to answer back."

From the way the man jogged quickly to his vehicle, Francis didn't think he'd been any comfort to him. *Ah, well.* People were so sensitive these days. Talking to one's pet wasn't *that* bizarre, was it?

As had been the case every day for the last few weeks, Francis found his feet suddenly walking down the street in a familiar direction. A left, a right and a few blocks were all it took to have them at Haddy's. It was absolutely pathetic.

Ruth waved when Francis walked by her bakery, nattering away on her phone. She paused to call out to him. "He's at the pub."

*Brilliant.*

Now Ruth would be on the phone to his gran to chunter on about how her grandson had gone to see Caddock again, and weren't they just the sweetest thing in the world. The two had probably already planned his wedding. *Honestly.* Nutters—the both of them—absolutely nutters. In other circumstances, he might find it endearing, in a demented sort of way.

"Looking for me, cub?" Caddock sprung up behind him, squeezing, then swatting his arse. "Did you bring me a coffee? I could use one. It's been a long morning already."

"No, I brought myself one." Francis attempted to stretch his arm out to prevent the theft of his coffee. Caddock had a longer reach and plucked it easily out of his hand. "*Oi.* Thief. Give it back."

"Coffee's bad for you." Caddock took a large gulp then grimaced. He glared at the cup as if it had deeply offended him. "I forgot you like a little coffee with your cream and sugar. This'll rot your teeth out. It's so sweet. How do you stand it?"

"Then why are you still drinking it?"

"Someone has to save you from yourself." He held the cup over his head away from Francis's reaching hands. He seemed highly amused by his greater reach. "See? Coffee stunts your growth. If you hadn't drunk so much, you might be able to grab it from me."

"Not everyone wants to be an overgrown brute." Francis slid his freezing fingers under the hem of Caddock's shirt. He enjoyed the warmth of his skin and the hiss of displeasure from Caddock. "Oh, dear, are my fingers icy cold? You've got warm coffee to help you out."

"You mercenary bastard." Caddock held out the coffee, but placed his own hand over Francis's to trap his fingers against his muscled abdomen. "I enjoy your touch."

"How on earth do you make words so innocent sound so filthy?" Francis laughed at the mischievous glint in Caddock's blue eyes. "Something they teach you on the rugby pitch?"

"Pure natural talent."

"There is *nothing* pure about you."

"Mornin'."

Francis snatched his hand away from Caddock's shirt when Father Williams, the village priest, walked by. "Good morning."

"You know, I can legally marry you both at the chapel anytime." The priest's eyes twinkled with merriment at what Francis was sure were shell-shocked looks in their eyes. "Have a good day now and the best of luck tomorrow evening."

"They do realize we've barely been together a month or so, right?" Francis rubbed his forehead with a resigned air of annoyance. He waved off Caddock's attempt to answer his rhetorical question. "The ground can come up to swallow me whole anytime now."

The entire village appeared to be in a competition to see how they could embarrass him the most. Francis's cheeks flushed a bright pink while Caddock simply chuckled. He should've stayed at home.

Caddock cupped the back of his neck to tug him up into a kiss. He used the distraction to grab Francis's coffee again. "My mother came by to take Devlin out for the day. Want to shag on the bar?"

"*Caddock.*" Francis shook his head with a laugh as he was dragged into the pub. "*Prat.*"

Sherlock danced around the two of them. His paws slipped

on the newly polished wooden floor. He immediately found the row of dog beds lining the far wall of the pub. Caddock had wanted to make the numerous dogs in the village as comfortable as their owners.

"He seems pleased with himself." Caddock moved over to the bar where he'd obviously been working on last minute paperwork. "If I'd known how much of this shit I'd have to deal with, I'm not sure I would've decided to own my own pub."

Francis followed him, hopping up onto the wooden bar. "Is it stretching your brain?"

"Oi, no lip from you." Caddock shoved the forms to the side. He caught Francis by the thigh to drag him down, and then moved to stand between his open legs. "You could make it up to me."

"Oh?"

He leaned in for a kiss. "This is a new pub after all. Perhaps we should christen it?"

"Windows...." Francis found his complaint swallowed by rough lips on his own. One touch turned into another and *another*. He finally pulled himself away remembering yet again how anyone looking in would see them. "*Caddock.*"

"There's always the upstairs office." He grinned wickedly. "But where's the fun in that?"

"Fun?" He had his doubts getting arrested would be considered enjoyable on any level. "It's not *exactly* sanitary either."

With an exaggerated groan, Caddock yanked him off the bar into his arms. He stalked out of the room and up the narrow stairs that lead to the office and storage space on the second floor of the building. He stumbled over a mop handle and they crashed to the floor.

Francis gave a pained groan from underneath the mass of the Brute. "Brilliant idea, truly."

"As soon as I've determined whether or not I've broken anything, I'm spanking you for your cheeky lack of faith in my abilities." Caddock flopped over with a sigh and ever so carefully twisted from side to side. "Fuck. I think I broke my back."

# Chapter Twenty-Nine

Despite the auspicious start to the day, the opening to the bar went spectacularly well. The evening flew by. Caddock barely had time to blink before he stood with his new staff cleaning up after they'd closed for the night with a till full to the brim with their earnings.

He'd done it.

Started his own pub.

And successfully opened to a full house.

On the heels of his bar opening, Caddock would've thought the worst of his stress to be over. He turned out to be wrong. His mother had thrown a wrench in his plans—dinner with the family, plus Francis and his gran.

How badly could it go? His father had claimed to have

changed. So really, how awful would it be for them all to eat together? His mother could keep an entire army in check; dealing with her husband should be a snap.

Fingers crossed the man had actually changed, else Caddock wouldn't be able to restrain himself if his father had a go at Francis. They'd be brawling in the back garden. And wouldn't it just make the evening so much better?

The visual in his mind might've been humorous if not for the tragic side of it. His mother would never forgive him if he ever struck his father. A lot rested on the way this turned out, so he hoped they were all up to the occasion.

Leaning against the sofa cushions, Caddock attempted to focus on the printouts from the sales at the pub for the first three days of business. He had expected day one to go well. The Brute come to Looe made Haddy's a novelty. He *hadn't* anticipated their success continuing as it had.

With luck, his pub would grow and grow. His young chef had experience in the kitchen and a hunger to make a name for himself. Caddock, after some consideration, decided to let him go for it. He'd given the young man complete control over the menu.

The food had been absolutely amazing—"fucking brilliant," according to Rupert. His old mate had been dragged in to taste test the day after the opening. Their lunch crowds almost exceeded the night-time numbers. They'd brought in a few servers to handle the workload.

When initially planning for the pub, Caddock had intended to have barely a skeleton crew. But after all the changes to the menu, he wouldn't cripple their efforts by not having the staff required. Hiring locally also endeared them to the village. It was good business all around.

Less than a week in might be too soon to claim success; Caddock, however, had a good feeling about it. Haddy's would be the silver lining to his forced retirement. It would be his *try* after the scrum. He would make it work.

"Uncle Boo? Can I watch *Owiver*? Can I? Pwease?" Devlin climbed up beside him on the couch, Blue the bear tucked safely under his arm. His nephew had watched one of the older versions of *Oliver* at least ten times in the last week. "You pwomised."

"Did I?" Caddock vaguely recalled foolishly saying the lad could see it again. *Shit.* It had taken ages to get the damn songs out of his head. "All right then, I can see it's time to torture your beloved uncle again."

Devlin giggled.

*Ahh, my little devilish sadist.*

He turned on the telly and set up the requested film. His eyes narrowed playfully on his nephew. "Cease your laughing or I'll toss you in the river in a sack."

"Gwannie would be cwoss with you," Devlin said with all the confidence of a four-year-old. "She'd put you on the naughty step with no cake."

"No cake? No cake! Oh no. How will I ever live in a world without it?" Caddock tickled his nephew, laughing at how much dessert ruled his world. "Your grandmother would never deny you cake—unless you dug up all her roses. I think she might love her flowers more than me. Maybe more than you."

"Uncle Boo."

Small hands batted away his poking fingers. Devlin had settled down after all the family drama. He thanked God for the hundredth time for the resilience of childhood.

His nephew began to sing along to the music on the telly. Caddock, to save his sanity, returned to the inventory lists his new chef had handed him the night before. They mostly sourced from local farms and shops. He liked the idea of repaying the community for its support.

"Is it lunch time yet, Uncle Boo?" Devlin paused in the middle of singing.

The one good thing about owning a pub with a brilliant chef: Caddock didn't have to live on beans on toast and waffles. Devlin had a one-track mind when it came to food. Children tended to be frustrating at times.

Devlin moved on from singing and considering lunch to having a serious debate with bear about who they loved more in the musical. It would be good when his primary school started up again. The lad needed other children to play with.

As the movie ended, Caddock packed up his paperwork. He took Devlin down to the pub for lunch. Anything to pull his mind away from the impending doom of the evening was preferable to sitting on the couch and brooding over it.

Time flew far too quickly for him. Supper with the family seemed to suddenly be upon them. If it hadn't been for the potential of hurting his mother's feelings, Caddock would've blown the whole thing off. For all his bluster, he could never stand to see her cry.

"You two are as tightly wound as a fiddle. I can feel my own eyes starting to twitch from *your* stress." Francis's gran,

Mrs Keen, stopped entertaining Devlin to speak to them. "Family is family, love."

"Very insightful, Gran." Francis sounded as anxious as Caddock felt. He reached out to hold Caddock's hand, wanting to offer comfort and wanting it for himself. "Family *is* family."

"Trust your gran. Everything will turn out all right." She went back to teaching Devlin one of the sea limericks he'd heard around town—one of the more child-friendly ones. She glanced over at the two silent men with a concerned frown. "What's the worst they can do? They're your parents."

"She's done it now. She's gone and jinxed us." Caddock groaned dramatically, sending his nephew into hysterical giggles. He glared over his shoulder at the lad. "It's always good to know you'll be there to laugh at my misfortune."

Upon arrival, Devlin took Mrs Keen by the sleeve to lead her into the house to meet his grandparents. They could hear his excited introductions all the way outside. Caddock stood beside Francis, reaching down to hold his hand while they drew in several calming breaths almost in unison.

"Ready then?" Francis sounded like they were about to take on a firing squad.

"No. But let's do it anyway." Caddock hadn't earned his reputation on the pitch for nothing. He always tended to do first then think afterwards. "Do you think my father might swoon if we snog at the dinner table? Might be worth it."

"*Caddock.*"

"Cub." Caddock deepened his voice in the way he knew always had an effect on Francis. He smirked when the hand in his suddenly tensed. "Something wrong?"

"You are a total and utter arse." Francis blocked him with his arm when Caddock attempted to swat him. "I refuse to sit at supper with our families with a sodding hard-on, so quit it. No getting handsy with me in your parents' house."

"I don't need to touch you to get a reaction though, do I?" Caddock bent forward so his breath rushed over his cub's ear. He saw the shivers run through Francis. "Shall we go inside? Or do you require a moment to settle yourself down?"

"Prat." Francis hissed at him in obvious annoyance. Caddock bent down to hush him with a kiss and used his hold on his hand to draw him closer. They separated after a few seconds, only to have Francis whack him on the arm. "Is this your idea of behaving? It's no wonder you spent so much time in the sin bin."

"My son has no concept of the word behave."

Caddock stiffened at the familiar voice. He turned towards the man, trying to casually place himself as a barrier between his father and his partner. "We were…."

He couldn't exactly tell his father what they'd been doing. For all his jokes, it wouldn't be wise to antagonize the man when he'd been making so much effort to change. Old dogs didn't learn new tricks easily.

"I'm Francis Keen, lovely to finally meet you—officially." He held out his hand expectantly, appearing completely calm except for the already fading pink on his neck and cheeks. "Thank you for welcoming my gran and me into your home. We've been looking forward to it."

Caddock's father stared blankly for a long, rather awkward moment before reaching out to shake Francis's hand. "I won't lie. I was fully prepared to *not* approve of you or this relationship. I had my mind set on being as difficult as a Stanford can be which is *incredibly*, obstinately bothersome."

"*Father.*"

"And I would've been wrong." His father gently patted the hand still resting in his own. "Forgive me for being an old fool. And please, it would be an honour to welcome you into our home *and* our family. My wife's told me what a lovely young man you are. I look forward to getting to know you myself."

"Thank you." Francis stumbled over his words, shocked at the sudden changes of mind. "Your grandson speaks highly of you."

The two men continued into the house. They left Caddock standing stunned by himself. Had Hell frozen over and no one bothered to tell him? He was well and truly gobsmacked.

He blinked when he realized they'd gone without him. "Oh, don't mind me then, I'm only your son."

"Do stop talking to yourself, Caddock. It won't do to have your young man thinking you're one step away from going batty." His mother looped her arm around his. She smiled up at him. "You look so amusingly bewildered. I did tell you he promised to behave himself."

"Yes, but…" Caddock hadn't believed true change could possibly come so quickly. He stood on the threshold of the living room, watching his father conversing easily with Francis and his grandmother. "…I hadn't dared to hope."

"You never do. You always were our little pessimist." She patted his arm fondly. "It's all right, dear. I have enough optimism for the entire Stanford clan."

# Chapter Thirty

Francis had a date to plan. Despite the numerous romantic classics he'd read over the years, it was *not* turning out to be a particular talent of his. Days went by with his mind remaining frustratingly blank on the subject.

He dithered. And then did it some more. At this point, Sherlock had better ideas than he did. Why was this so bloody difficult? Restoring an eighteenth-century painting had been easier.

The answer finally came to him while straightening up toys and books on a visit to Devlin and Caddock. A letter had been stuck in *The Wind in the Willows*. It appeared to be an invitation to an awards ceremony in which the Brute would be receiving special recognition for his years of service to English Rugby.

*Interesting.*

It was scheduled for the following week. Why hadn't Caddock at least mentioned it to him? They spoke about everything else. He didn't for a second believe the man was ashamed of their relationship.

Caddock flaunted the fact that they were a couple. It likely had nothing to do with him and everything to do with rugby being a sensitive subject. This had potential.

A note attached to it indicated Caddock had refused to attend. Francis's mind immediately began to go into overdrive. He could understand not wanting to be in some impersonal hotel ballroom with hundreds of people staring at him.

Caddock had gone through so much turmoil towards the end of his career. It didn't mean the man wouldn't enjoy feeling appreciated by those who played beside him. Francis wondered if there might be a better way to go about it than a posh banquet that the players, for the most part, would hate.

Making his excuses, Francis quickly bailed on Caddock and Devlin. Time to find someone who excelled at plotting behind others' backs. He would definitely need help with this, since his knowledge of the rugby world tended to revolve around how well their arses look in those tight shorts.

Rupert might not be prone to keeping his mouth shut when secrets were involved, but he did have the in when it came to Caddock's world of sport. The two men had played together for years. It also didn't hurt that the man tended to be up for anything that might even slightly resemble a prank. And pulling one over the Brute's eyes would certainly fit the bill.

They met up at Rupert's realtor office, since anyone interrupting would assume the conversation was about a new design job. Francis showed him the invitation he'd nicked. Rupert immediately agreed to attempt to put together something a tad more personal to celebrate.

Of course, it then took another hour to reel in Rupert's wilder ideas. They finally seized on the idea of a charity rugby match in the Brute's honour, maybe something in support of preservation of the Great Barrier Reef—a cause close to Haddy's heart. The award could be presented prior to the game.

The theory was Caddock might more gracefully accept it on friendlier footing. It might work. Maybe it wasn't a romantic night out, but this was about who they were as a couple and individuals.

"The Brute'll be pissed at first," Rupert said casually, but in clear warning. "A few snogs'll set him straight."

Francis pierced him with a hard stare. "Pun intended? You *will* resist the urge to prod at him about this. Do you understand? Caddock will be prickly enough without you being your normally exhausting self. Just remember, I know your wife and she likes me better than you."

"Only because you bribed her with a sodding tea set," Rupert muttered grumpily. "Do you know how hard I had to work to find a Christmas present to top it? Bloody bone china. It's so delicate, she gets all cross with me if I dare to touch it with my *man* hands."

Francis had a chuckle at the man's expense. Joanne loved

all things delicate and floral. He had been on one of his antique hunts when he'd stumbled across a pale blue tea set from the early eighteen hundreds. It had been a thank you for all the nights he'd spent in their guest room. The couple really had been rather amazing friends to him.

"Oh, poor Rupert." Francis threw a pen at him and then grew serious. "Do you think he'll hate me for this?"

"Yes."

"*Brilliant*." He didn't want this to turn into a spectacle that would upset Francis. "Maybe we shouldn't."

Rupert's smile evaporated when he realized how worried Francis truly was about his boyfriend's reaction. "Caddock will probably want to shag you senseless by way of thanks. Ha! You blushed. Listen, Francis, the man is beyond infatuated with you. He'll go all warm and gooey inside at the effort you're going to for him. It'll be dreadfully sickening. I'll be sure to have buckets nearby for anyone reduced to vomiting."

"Lovely visuals, thanks. Also, you're an idiot." Francis did feel slightly less panicky over the plans. "Can you call your old teammates and manager about this? They might think I'm a crazed fan if I do it."

"Of course."

The two quickly ironed out the rest of the details. Francis would convince Caddock to go into London for an afternoon out with Devlin. Rupert would organize everything for their families to get to the stadium. The hardest part would be keeping the media from catching wind of it.

Charity rugby events with the *entire* former and current English National Team in attendance would be big news.

They could only pray that even if the tabloids learned of the match perhaps they wouldn't know the real reason behind it. Maybe the press would simply think it was yet another random sporting event.

"Be sure to distract Caddock with plenty of blow jobs—it works for Joanne." Rupert moved over to pour himself a glass of water instead of Scotch, in deference to Francis. "What? Stop frowning at me."

Francis flushed several shades of pink while spluttering for a moment. He decided to settle on annoyed instead of embarrassed. "I'm quite certain Joanne wouldn't appreciate you blithely sharing the details of your sexual deviances with me."

"If you consider a blow job sexual deviance, Caddock has much to educate you on." He pulled his legs quickly out of reach of the bag Francis slung at him. "Now, now, there's no need to resort to violence. You should really learn to broaden your horizons."

Francis decided it was time to return home, and then remembered the other reason he'd wanted to visit. "Oh, next time you have new clients, don't send me the batty old couples who think putrid ochre goes with vomit green."

"Are those actual colours?" Rupert paled at the descriptions. "I thought you loved eccentrics—particularly since you are one."

"This"—Francis gestured towards himself—"is my unamused face. You should fear and avoid it."

"See? Eccentrically British at its best."

"I'm going to leave now." He allowed Rupert to pull him

212

into a hug when he got to his feet. "Careful, my oddness might be contagious."

Rupert released him with a wry chuckle. "You wouldn't be you without a hint of uniqueness."

"I can never tell if you mean that in a good or a bad way." Francis shook his head and decided to leave before he provided the man with another reason to tease him.

The ride home was uneventful, aside from Sherlock, who insisted on informing him with loud barks about the cars trailing behind Watson. Francis had a feeling Rupert's secretary might've fed him one too many dog treats. He rarely went on and on like this.

"Sherlock, is it *really* necessary to have a go at every single car?" Francis could feel a migraine growing already. He winced when a passing Volvo set his dog off again. "I'll tell Ruth to stop making your biscuits for an entire week. I will. I'll even tell her not to say hello."

Blissful silence.

The threat kept Sherlock quiet the whole way home. Gran took one look at him when they arrived and bundled him off to bed with a hot compress. He stayed there for the rest of the day, not even bothering with tea or supper. The simple act of lifting his head made him distinctly nauseous.

A gentle touch woke Francis late in the evening. He could tell from way the moonlight shone into his room that the sun had been down for a while. The pain in his head had blissfully faded.

"You look like shite." Caddock lifted the now dry cloth from his forehead. "How's your head?"

"Better. Did we have plans?" Francis couldn't remember making any with him. "And I do not look dreadful enough for your foul language—thanks ever so much."

"Devlin wanted to see Sherlock," Caddock answered casually. He brushed his fingers gently through Francis's sleep-mussed hair. "And I wanted to see you."

Sternly telling himself not to read deeper things into such an innocent turn of phrase, Francis sat up in bed. He shoved the blankets away from his chest. It was honestly surprising Caddock had been able to get into his room.

With a surprisingly gentle touch, Caddock began to massage Francis's scalp. He wilted into his pillow. Those last few lingering aches from his migraine dissipated with each passing second.

"Rupert said you paid him a visit."

"Did he?" Francis closed his eyes; feigning sleep seemed a good way to go.

"He did. He wouldn't tell me why, claimed it was about a new client." Caddock lifted his hands away then tapped Francis on the nose until he opened his eyes. "The thing is, Joanne told me Rupert had a slow week with no new clients. What are you two up to?"

"We're trying to figure out a way to convince you and Joanne to agree to a wild orgy." Francis impressed himself with his own ability to maintain a straight face. He didn't even crack a smile. "They are a rather attractive couple."

Caddock's eyebrows rose high on his forehead. "An orgy? You?"

He mock glared. "Are you calling me a prude?"

214

# After the Scrum

"Not a prude. But you do blush if I so much as grab your arse in sight of anyone. How do you plan on having an orgy?" Caddock asked dubiously. "Fine, fine. Keep your secrets. Rupert'll spill the beans to me eventually, probably over a pint or four."

Francis didn't bother disagreeing since he wasn't exactly wrong. *Time to play dirty.* "It's a surprise. Please don't ruin it."

Blue eyes met slightly pleading blue eyes. Francis refused to back down. He'd never planned something to this scale—curiosity would *not* be permitted to screw up all his work.

"Uncle Boo?" Devlin peeked around the door. He bounced into the room with Sherlock on his heels. They both climbed up onto the bed. "Can we have tea?"

"Did you invite yourself or did Mrs Keen invite us?" Caddock winked at Francis before turning a stern glaze on his nephew. "Well?"

"I invited you both. So how about you get out of my grandson's bed?" Gran waved a wooden spoon at the group. "Who wants scones?"

"*Me!*" Devlin leapt from the bed, almost catching his head on the nearby desk. He careened down the hall. "Scones, Uncle Boo, scones."

"Was he by chance the sprog of a jumping bean?" Francis found all the exuberant energy exhausting.

"Only a third." Caddock got to his feet then caught Francis when he stumbled, his legs caught by the quilt. "C'mon, Fwannie, I could eat a horse."

"You are only half as funny as you think you are."

# Chapter Thirty-One

When Joanne had mentioned Rupert and Francis had been holed up in his office for a while, Caddock had figured the two were plotting something. He hadn't bothered about it much. It would all come out eventually, after all.

And it had.

He had been well and truly surprised. Francis had convinced him they were about to have a simple picnic at the stadium. Seeing every player he'd ever worked with on the pitch had blown him away.

Now, standing beside the national team manager who was handing him a bizarrely sculpted statue that honoured his professional achievements, Caddock found himself more emotional than anticipated. He blinked back tears. It touched him to realise he hadn't been forgotten.

While everyone gathered around tables filled with tiny bites of food, Rupert pulled him aside to explain how Francis had worked his slender fingers to the bone to make sure it all went without a hitch. It had been his idea from the start. And everything had been done to make the day special for him.

As the others began to run mock games with each other and their kids who'd attended, Caddock worked his way through the crowd. He found his cub in the middle of a conversation with one of his old training coaches. And not one he particularly liked.

It reminded him of a promise he'd once made. The assistant trainer had an overly swanky office at the stadium. He had a smarmy attitude to go with it. They had butted heads almost constantly.

The man had gone out of his way to screw Caddock over so often, he'd always wanted to return the favour. Francis would look wonderfully decadent bent over the man's desk. It seemed he'd finally gotten his chance.

"Someone is thinking naughty thoughts." Francis watched him apprehensively out of the corner of his eye. He hadn't said anything earlier when Caddock grabbed him to lead him away from pitch. "What are you up to? I can almost hear the deviant wheels turning in your mind. We're not going to get arrested, are we? My gran's here, so are you parents."

Caddock kept firm hands on Francis's shoulders, guiding him down the familiar tunnel that led to a row of doors. "I thought you deserved a physical demonstration of my gratitude for all you did for me today."

"You're using big words. Should I be afraid now?" He glanced over his shoulder with a cheeky smile. "Are we going to create a scandal on your special day? I'm sure the tabloid reporters would love it."

For all the teasing, Caddock could feel the shoulders under his fingers tensing. He massaged them gently. It would be a fun-filled afternoon, but he'd never risk exposing Francis at all.

Doors had locks.

Knowing time would be of the essence, Caddock sped up the pace. They finally found the right door. He snuck inside with Francis then immediately secured the door behind them.

"What are we doing?"

Caddock leaned against the door for a moment, simply watching Francis grow ever more uneasy under scrutiny. He loved the bow ties the man wore. It always made him want to yank it off, use it to keep him quiet or bind his hands. He'd never imagined a single strip of fabric could bring such lurid fantasies out of him.

His patience came to an end. Two steps and they were toe to toe. Francis stumbled back in surprise against the desk when his bow tie was ripped off his body.

"Not my colour?"

"On the contrary." Caddock caught him by the wrists and bound them behind his back. He paused, maintaining eye contact. "If it makes you uncomfortable, I'll release you immediately."

"The only uncomfortable part of me happens to be the tight restriction of my trousers." Francis bucked forward against the thigh Caddock pushed between his legs. "Why this office?"

"Revenge."

They didn't have time for words. Or finesse. Trousers and pants were shoved down to their ankles faster than he thought possible. Caddock spun Francis around after one hard kiss. He pressed him gently on top of the desk, pausing to take in the view he made.

He encountered the shock of his life a moment later. "Are you…?"

"Wearing one of those plugs you thought I hadn't noticed in your closet?"

"Bloody hell. Have you been wearing it all day?" Caddock tapped his finger against the plastic base, causing Francis to let out a loud moan. "Been holding that one in have you? How on earth have you had this in and I didn't notice? And you call me a kinky bastard."

"You are one." Francis craned his neck to peer back at him. "Had a feeling you'd want to do something like this. I thought being—"

"Lubed and loosened?"

Francis dropped his head forward to the desk. "Must you be so blunt?"

"Yes."

He worked the toy in and out several times, wanting Francis to be right on the edge. His eyes strayed to the clock on the wall. They had maybe fifteen minutes before their absence became painfully obvious.

Voices in the hall had him quieting Francis with his hand over his mouth. Caddock continued teasing him though. He found nothing quite like the adrenaline rush from *almost* being discovered to add head to the moment.

Removing the well-lubed toy, Caddock wrapped it in a handkerchief and stowed it in his jacket pocket. It wouldn't be wise to accidentally leave it somewhere. He dipped his fingers into Francis once or twice, prolonging his own enjoyment, and then grabbed a condom from one of the pockets of his trousers.

He sensed Francis growing closer to his completion. "Are you ready, cub? Ready for me?"

Keeping an ear listening for any chatter in the hall, Caddock gripped Francis firmly by the waist and guided him back. He bent forward to bite and suck on a spot on his back to silence his own groans. Nothing felt more brilliant than thrusting into his Francis.

*Absolutely fucking brilliant.*

Reaching around to take a hold of Francis, Caddock stroked him in time with his movements. The slight tightening around him sent little shockwaves of pleasure through him. Francis had clearly been on the edge for hours. It took next to no time for him find his glimpse of heaven.

The man clenched around him like a damn vise. Caddock gritted his teeth to keep from shouting. His orgasm was wrung from him sooner than he would've liked.

He slowly lifted himself off Francis. "We can sneak to the loo to clean up. It's a few doors down."

Francis held up a rather moist sheet of paper. "I appear to have ruined the roster for next week."

Caddock blinked at him several times then threw his head

back to roar with laughter. "I'm tempted to tell you to leave it for the bastard to find, but he might have coppers do a forensic test. C'mon, we'll toss it in a rubbish bin with my condom."

"Lovely."

A quick wash-up in the club showers and the two looked good as new. Slightly rumpled, but nothing anyone should notice. Caddock grinned smugly at Francis, who rolled his eyes in response.

"You didn't." Rupert stopped them at the end of the tunnel on their way back to join the party. "You didn't. You did. You randy buggers."

"Me? I'm sure a prude like myself has no idea what you're on about." Francis stared blankly at him, though his flushed neck gave him away. "You do have the most *vivid* imagination."

Rupert reached out with a napkin to pointedly wipe one of Francis's jacket sleeves. "Might want to check yourself in the mirror next time."

Francis covered his face with his hands. "Anyone mind if I die here?"

"I do." Caddock elbowed Rupert hard in the side. "Go bother your wife. Leave my Francis alone."

"I'm never going out again." Francis refused to lift his head from his hands.

Caddock laughed at Francis's obvious embarrassment. He pulled him into his arms. "Thank you. Not sure where my life would be without you. Dull and empty, I'm sure."

# Epilogue

*"Get your arse to the pub. All hell broke loose."*

Francis had been in the middle of working on the restoration of a nineteenth-century china cabinet. He'd found it on a farm a few villages over. It needed a bit of love and would look good as new; maybe not new, but close enough to sell for four times what he'd paid for it.

The panicked call from the chef at the pub sent him racing for the door. Francis had been on the man's call list for a year now. Caddock tended to pretend his mobile didn't exist much of the time.

# After the Scrum

They'd been living together for the last six months. Francis had been hesitant at first. He'd thought a year and a half might be too soon in a relationship. But one of his gran's friends had come to stay, and they were a bit much for him.

Devlin greatly enjoyed having his Francis and his Sherlock at the cottage. The seven-year-old had grown like a weed. He had readily accepted the two men as a couple, and his enthusiasm had helped smooth the edges with his grandfather.

The family regularly got together without so much as a raised eyebrow. Francis found himself amazed at the difference two years had made in his life. His design business had moved into antique restoration. It was more satisfying and financially rewarding.

Francis pulled Watson up outside the pub, rushing in with Sherlock close behind. He stopped dead centre in the middle of the room when he realized Caddock was kneeling in front of him. Their friends and family had gathered around them in a semicircle.

"What…?"

"Father Williams tells me it's all legal." Caddock stayed on one knee. He retrieved a black box from his front pocket, opening it to reveal a single platinum band with a dark blue line running through the centre. "Will you marry me?"

"Pardon?"

Caddock caught him by the hand to drag him closer when Francis froze in place. He slid the ring on his finger. "I know your brilliant mind will catch up sooner or later. Shall I assume the answer is yes?"

"You presumptuous prat." He sternly told himself that

blubbering in front of everyone would be humiliating. He blinked rapidly before finally glancing away from the ring on his finger to the man on his knees. "You could've waited for my yes."

"True." He got to his feet with a pained grimace. His old injury had been flaring up recently. "I thought I'd speed things along a bit for everyone's benefit."

A cheer went up around the gathered crowd. Francis found himself hugged and kissed by everyone. His grandmother had tears in her eyes—happy tears, she promised. She immediately wandered over to begin a discussion with Ruth and Caddock's mother, likely about wedding plans.

Francis barely restrained a shiver at the insanity that would likely develop. Maybe they should elope? He'd talk to Caddock about it later.

"Are you happy?"

Francis lifted his eyes from his engagement ring. He'd been staring at it for a good ten minutes. He found Caddock's father before him. "I am. I love your son. I believe we have every chance of being quite happily married."

Arthur Stanford nodded solemnly at him. "He's a good man. I worried about him. He never settled like Hadrian. My Hadrian. He could've been a carbon copy of me. I've never understood Caddock. But I love him. I wanted him to find happiness."

"Most fathers want their children to be happy." Francis wondered apprehensively where this conversation was going. He spun the ring on his finger absently. "Are you concerned he won't be?"

# After the Scrum

Arthur broke into a broad smile, reminding Francis of a picture he'd seen of Hadrian. "Not at all. I wanted to wish you congratulations. And to thank you for bringing my son such joy. He struggled after his injury. You helped prod him into returning to himself. Welcome to our family."

The hug Arthur dragged him into was *all* Caddock. Crushingly hard embraces apparently ran in the family. Having had his say, the man disappeared into the crowd, likely to find a drink and gain some semblance of his usually austere self.

"Everything all right?"

Francis smiled at his fiancé. "Coming to rescue me?"

"Did you need it?"

"Not even close. He welcomed me to the family." Francis thought it had been rather sweet of the man actually. "He wanted to know if I love you."

"Oh? Did he?" Caddock sounded as if he couldn't imagine his father actually asking. "What did you say?"

He smiled at the overly casual question. "Told him to bugger off with his nosy, priggish attitude."

"*Francis.*"

He laughed so hard he had to grab Caddock to keep from falling to the floor. "If you could see your face! I said I love you, silly prat."

Caddock leaned in close, letting his rough lips graze against Francis's ear. "I love you. So much so, I'm going to punish you later for teasing me."

His heart sped up at the thought. The two usually had a lot of fun with supposed punishments. It was a silly game, but it kept life interesting.

Caddock's large hands came up to frame his face. His thumb caressed Francis's stubble-covered cheek. "I do love you so incredibly much. I've had the ring for months."

"Had to find the nerve?"

"No, no, I wanted it all to be perfect." Caddock bent down to capture his lips in a kiss that had their friends whistling encouragement. "You'll be pleased to know Devlin helped me pick out the ring."

"Smart lad."

"Takes after his uncle."

Francis found himself yanked out of Caddock's embrace before he could respond. "*Oi.*"

"What? Were you busy?" Rupert gave him a bone-crushing hug of his own. "So, who's your best man going to be?"

"Sherlock."

"What am I? Chopped liver?" Rupert steadily led him across the bar. "I'm hurt."

"You're more like chopped toad." Francis glanced over his shoulder, but Caddock was lost in a sea of villagers. "Where are we going?"

"Do people eat chopped toad?" He grimaced in disgust then brightened again. "I have a surprise for you."

The surprise turned out to be Graham, home from yet another overseas assignment. The three of them escaped up into the upstairs office with Caddock following a few minutes later. They sat on the floor in a circle, trading stories and enjoying a bottle of non-alcoholic cider between them.

"My wife has joined in the wedding-planning madness," Rupert warned them after they'd finished the cider. "It's going to be the Looe event of the century."

"How long would it take to get to Gretna Green?" Francis wondered absently.

"Do people still do that? Can't you just go to the registrar's office?" Graham opened the second bottle he'd hidden by the door. "Or better yet, Father Williams adores you. He'd marry you in a trice."

While the others argued about the best way to get married without a circus, Francis leaned his head against Caddock's broad shoulder. He blushed when he caught sight of a ripped bow tie in the corner of the room. It had been missing for weeks. Must've been left over from one of their "christening the office" nights out.

"We could get married tonight." Caddock plucked a licence out of his pocket, waving it in front of Francis's face. "Everyone's here, even the priest."

"Brilliant." He turned towards Rupert. "You get to tell everyone."

"Why me?"

"Because you're the one who told everyone in the village I got Caddock's name tattooed on my arse." Francis waved the cider bottle at him threateningly. He *hadn't* gotten anything tattooed on his arse or anywhere else. He hated needles. "Do you know how many times Gran whacked me on the head with a spoon?"

Rupert grinned unrepentantly at him. "How do you know I won't embellish things while I'm telling them the wedding is happening tonight?"

"Because I'll tell your wife it was your idea, and you

were the one who robbed her of the pleasure of planning our ceremony." He threatened the man with the only thing known to cow him into behaving—Joanne. "Good luck. We'll be down momentarily."

"No shagging on the desk again or I'll send your gran up to find you." Rupert caught his brother by the arm to pull him from the room with him. "You've got five minutes."

Francis wandered over to snag the torn tie from the floor. He shoved it into his pocket. It wouldn't do for one of the pub workers to find it and wonder where it came from. He found his soon-to-be husband watching him seriously. "Are you really ready?"

Caddock reached into his jacket to retrieve a second jewellery box. "I brought these with me, just in case."

"Was this a surprise proposal or a surprise wedding?" He wouldn't put it past the man to plan out the easiest, least stressful way to get married possible. "Am I becoming Mr Stanford-Keen? Or Mr Stanford?"

"Either, neither? I'm not all wound up on you changing your name. I only want you to be mine." Caddock looped his arm around his fiancé's waist to pull him over. "I think I fell in love with you when you nattered on to Sherlock about which biscuit was his and which was mine."

"*Caddock*." Francis could feel the flush growing on his neck. "You fell in love when you realized I was absolutely nutty?"

Caddock kissed him roughly, deep voice gruffer than normal. "I love you—couldn't love you more if I tried. Marry me? Here in the pub where it all started?"

228

# After the Scrum

"You thought I was a woman." Francis remembered their first meeting with a fond smile. He'd never imagined how one new client could alter his entire world. "I never dreamed I would be able to marry."

"So?"

"Yes, I will marry you."

# The End.

# Acknowledgements

I'd like to thank my brilliant betas who keep me from losing my mind, Becky and all the brilliant people at Hot Tree, and my beloved hubby who didn't complain too much about all the rugby I was watching—for research purposes of course.

And lastly, a massive thank you to anyone who reads this story.

I hope you enjoy my precious boys as much as I did in writing them.

# About the Author

Dahlia Donovan wrote her first romance series after a crazy dream about shifters and damsels in distress. She prefers irreverent humour and unconventional characters.

An autistic and occasional hermit, her life wouldn't be complete without her husband and her massive collection of books and video games.

Stay connected with Dahlia:

Facebook: Facebook.com/DahliaDonovan

Website: www.DahliaDonovan.com

Twitter: Twitter.com/DahliaDonovan

# About the Publisher

Hot Tree Publishing opened its doors in 2015 with an aspiration to bring quality fiction to the world of readers. With the initial focus on romance and a wide spread of romance sub-genres, we envision opening up to alternative genres in the near future.

Firmly seated in the industry as a leading editing provider to independent authors and small publishing houses, Hot Tree Publishing is the sister company to Hot Tree Editing, founded in 2012. Having established in-house editing and promotions, plus having a well-respected market presence, Hot Tree Publishing endeavours to be a leader in bringing quality stories to the world of readers.

Interested in discover more amazing reads brought to you by Hot Tree Publishing or perhaps you're interesting in submitting a manuscript and joining the HTPubs family? Either way, head over to the website for information:

*www.HotTreePublishing.com*

54942063R00145

Made in the USA
Charleston, SC
14 April 2016